ROBERT WESTALL

The Stones of Muncaster Cathedral

Two stories of the supernatural

PENGUIN BOOKS

For my good friend Jessica Yates

CS04691699

PENGUIN BOOKS

Published by the Penguin Group
Penguin Books Ltd, 27 Wrights Lane, London W8 5TZ, England
Penguin Books USA Inc., 375 Hudson Street, New York, New York 10014, USA
Penguin Books Australia Ltd, Ringwood, Victoria, Australia
Penguin Books Canada Ltd, 10 Alcorn Avenue, Toronto, Ontario, Canada M4V 3B2
Penguin Books (NZ) Ltd, 182–190 Wairau Road, Auckland 10, New Zealand

Penguin Books Ltd, Registered Offices: Harmondsworth, Middlesex, England

First published by Viking 1991
Published in Penguin Books 1993
1 3 5 7 9 10 8 6 4 2

The moral right of the author has been asserted

Printed in England by Clays Ltd, St Ives plc
Filmset in Monophoto Garamond

Contents

The Stones of
Muncaster Cathedral

I never had any fear of heights.

I climbed my first factory chimney when I was four years old. My granda took me up. We were out for a ride, and we came to this site where my dad was working, and my granda said did I want to climb up to him, so I went. Granda was right behind me, wi' an arm on the ladder each side o' me, but he needn't ha' bothered. To me it was just a grand game. When I got to my dad up top, I felt like a bird, like a king.

We took my own lad, Kevin, up top, when he was four. He thought nowt to it either. None of our family ever has. Steeplejacks for five generations; Josiah Clarke and Sons.

I can still ladder-up a chimney in three hours, including hammering in our own wedges to hold the ladders. Over the years you can tell a wedge is going to hold, by the ringing of the brick as you drive the wedge in. Then we check the chimney top for cracks, the iron bands for rust, the lightning conductor for corrosion. Cost you two hundred quid. I'll do you a cooling tower, a town hall ...

But no more cathedrals. Not after Muncaster.

Mind you, I was chuffed when we first got Muncaster. A cathedral job is to a steeplejack what a canon's stall is to a vicar. I'm not a religious man, but it's the status, you see.

I mind the day I first heard about the Muncaster job. I'd just felled a chimney at the old brickworks. There's nowt to felling a chimney – it's a day's work, and it'll cost you four hundred and a hell of a lot for insurance. But I can fell a hundred-foot chimney into a twenty-two-foot gap, no sweat. The hardest part is agreeing with the chimney's owner exactly where he wants it to fall. Then you get your mate to stand there, and line you up, while you draw your chalk marks on the chimney base. Then you cut two holes in the base – the pneumatic drill cuts the old brick like cheese – and leave a brick pillar in between to hold the chimney up.

Then you drill the pillar to take the gelignite, and tamp it in wi' balls of clay. That's the weird thing, the jelly kicks against the hardness of the stack, not the softness of the clay. You mask the place wi' old railway sleepers against the odd flying brick, wire up the charge ... and bingo. There isn't much of a bang.

Funny, a standing chimney's like a man, upright and hard and rigid. But a falling chimney lies down like a woman, supple as a whip. Just gives a little hop off her base, then starts to fall, segmenting as she comes, then down wi' a thud and a smoke and there's no more harm in her. But if she should hit some overhead wires on the way down, say, it'd be enough to make her change direction and leap at you like a tiger. It's easy enough to forget overhead wires, if you're not careful.

Anyway, that day me and my mate Billy had laid the stack between a working brick factory and a transformer that had cost the electric board a cool hundred thousand, and done it sweet as a nut, not a broken window.

Then my wife phoned the brickworks with the news about Muncaster. I couldn't believe my ears.

'What about Barrass Brothers?' I yelped. 'They always do the cathedral.'

'Busy at Gloucester all summer. Big job,' she says.

'What about Munday and Lewis?' I couldn't believe my luck. Cathedrals were for the big boys.

'They say Jack Munday's hurt his back on the town hall job.'

I believed her; I believed Jack Munday and the Barrass Brothers, the lying sods. I never dreamt they might know something I didn't.

'What's the job?'

'South-west tower. Rotten stone and the weathercock needs seeing to.'

'Fair enough.' We do gilding an' brazing, as well as masonry. Jacks of all trades, steeplejacks. And masters of them, too.

The next Monday morning, I went round to the cathedral masons' yard, to see Taffy Evans, the foreman. Got a lot in common, steeplejacks and masons. Understand the stone, and the tools. But masons like to keep their feet on something solid. When it comes to lowering yourself down from the top of a steeple in a rope-cradle, masons aren't that interested. You can make a living as a mason, if you've got no head for heights at all.

'Got the key to the north-west tower, Taff?'

'South-west you want, boy. Nothing wrong with the north-west.'

'Just want to go and look,' I said, showing him the binoculars in my bag. 'There's things you can see from a distance you don't always spot close-to.'

He gave me some kind of old-fashioned look, though I couldn't make out what sort, cos he was wearing a face-mask against the stone-dust. I swear he was going to say something to me; but at that moment one of his apprentices started using the stone-saw, and it was impossible for him to say anything at all. I just took the key, and got away from the devil's racket of the stone-carving shop, and went off up the narrow dark winding stairs of the north-west tower. It was quiet and soothing; just the distant noise of the cathedral organist practising a voluntary. There was never anything wrong with the north-west tower.

Through the binoculars, which brought everything up closer than life, there didn't seem a lot wrong with the south-west tower either. Some rotten blocks in the stone steeple that would need cutting out and replacing. And the gilding on the weathercock was dull and thin, where the weather had been at it. And the cock turned poorly and stiffly on its vane. Much longer, and it would be seized up solid. Nothing we couldn't handle.

I was just lowering the binoculars when a stone face swam up, peering back at me, and something made me focus again.

There were a cluster of gargoyles on both the west towers, where the towers ended, and the stone steeples began. Funny things gargoyles; carved in the shape of devils and monkeys and men with toothache. The men who carved them centuries ago made them look as evil as they could, evil enough to frighten real devils away. And sometimes the wear and tear of wind and rain has made them look more evil today than when they were carved. They never worried me; just honest stone and the work of men's hands, and the work of wind and frost and rain.

But this one; it really looked as if it was watching me. I spent ten minutes with the binoculars watching it back. Then I told myself it was just stone, and the work of men's hands and the wind and the frost, and not to be so bloody stupid.

Anyway, that's what I told myself at the time.

There were just two of us on the job, me and Billy Simpson. Billy was my special mate – I didn't feel so sure of my other fellers. But Billy fixed my sling, and I fixed his, and we trusted each other. A new chap, you never trust him for about two years – till you know by heart what he's going to do next. Death isn't in the stone, however treacherous, or the height; death's inside the head of some bloke whose mind's not on his job. Stone is just stone ...

Except, well, the moment we got on to the spiral stair of the south-west tower, I didn't like it. It didn't feel the same as the north-west tower. The stair seemed narrower, as we lugged the ropes and pulley up; the lancet windows seemed to let in less light. The stone seemed darker, with a bloom of damp on it.

Bloody hell, I told myself, snap out of it. These two towers is exactly the same, identical twins. It's the Froggies who build their two west towers different. Snap out of it, Joe Clarke, admit you had one too many lagers watching the telly last night. Don't go on like a wet girl ...

And yet I couldn't seem to focus my eyes properly; the darkness seemed to lift off the surface of the stone and float in the air like smoke, so that I shook my head to clear it.

I didn't like it. Steeplejacking and emotions just don't go together. I employ steady fellers who are happily married with nice kids. Up there, a feller with another woman, or a debt, or maintenance payments on his mind, is a killer.

We got the hoist rigged up over the parapet, and waited for Tommy Small the apprentice to turn up with the main gear in the pick-up. It was a lovely morning, blue from horizon to horizon, but with a nice little breeze, not too hot. We leaned on the parapet and had a smoke and watched the town. Towns look a lot different from up top; you see a lot more. You see a lot that people don't expect you to see; you can give them some surprises. Like the time we were doing St Stephen's at Wallchurch, which is right next to the church school. And this young teacher was marching the kids in from the playground, class by class. Only he picked on this little lad, he was about eight, just our Kevin's age. Kept him behind when the rest had marched in, and went on at him till he cried. Then he clouted him for crying.

Me and Billy went down and had a few words wi' the headmaster, an' he had the young teacher in, and faced him with it. He was fair amazed, hadn't even realized we'd been up there watching him; though all the kids knew we were there. He got the sack soon after, I'm glad to say.

But height can play funny tricks. When we were doing the clock tower at Middleham, there was this bird sitting reading a book in the town square. Billy reckoned she was a right stunner; I reckoned not. We argued so much, we went all the way down to see. She was about sixty-five, though Billy said I couldn't prove it cos I didn't actually ask her. Well, you couldn't, could you?

But I had the laugh on him, cos I invited him to chat her up, and you've never seen anyone get back to scaffolding so quick.

That morning, there was already a little half-circle of people watching us. Sometimes, when you're doing something spectacular, the circle gets really thick; people with cameras and binoculars even. Other times, only a few. But there's always somebody there. Height seems to fascinate people. A surprising number want to come right up to the top with you, just for the kicks. Architects, clergy, pretty girls. You can't take the pretty girls, because of the insurance, more's the pity.

But once they're up there, they all want to hold on to something with one hand. They would never make steeplejacks. Steeplejacks have to stand up there and let go wi' both hands. You can't do your work holding on wi' one all the time.

Anyway, we're standing there smoking, when Billy catches sight o' that gargoyle.

'Just look at that,' he says. I thought it a bit odd it should affect him that way as well. I mean, gargoyles are no more to us than a water tap is to you.

'Ugly sod, isn't he?' I said.

'It's not that. Look at that flippin' stone.'

I turned to look with him. 'Good as the day it was carved,' I said. 'And five hundred years old, if it's a day.' You can tell: no Victorian or modern mason could carve a real lively gargoyle, they always look wooden somehow. I suppose you can only carve a decent gargoyle if you believe in real devils, and we don't now.

'Not the gargoyle, the stone around it. It's as rotten as mouldy cheese.'

The life of stone varies, you see. It doesn't last for ever just because it's stone. If it's the wrong stone, or wrongly laid, it can be up the spout in twenty years.

We got two kinds of sandstone round here, Bunter and Keuper. The old masons loved the rose-red Bunter, cos it carved so easily an' well. Trouble is, over the years, it dissolves like sugar-cubes. Pity the parish church council whose church is made of Bunter: their hands is never out of their pockets.

Keuper's not so pretty and it's stubborn work to carve; starts off yellowy-brown and then goes black wi' the soot in the air. But it grows a hard black skin and then it'll last for ever.

But even Keuper will go if you bed it wrong. If you bed it with the layers vertical, the rain and frost will slice them off like a bacon-slicer. Bed the layers horizontal, and the frost will just slowly nibble at their ends over the centuries.

We looked at the rotten stone around the gargoyle.

'It's Keuper OK; and bedded right. And it's not that old, look at them stone-saw marks . . .'

But I dug in my thumb-nail, and it came away in great chunks like cake, yellow under the black outer skin. 'That's not weatherin' . . .'

'I'll tell you somethin' else,' said Billy. 'It's been renewed since the last War, cos there's my Uncle Jim's mark, clear as clear.'

I looked at the little mark, a bit like a fish-hook. It was his Uncle Jim's mark, all right. In the old days, every mason left his mark scratched on his handiwork. Some still do it.

'Jim didn't finish serving his time till 1957 . . .'

'This stone's thirty-three years old at the most, an' no more use than fossilized shit.'

'Look at the way the rot's spread! Above, underneath, each side ... how far do you think it's gone? Inside?'

We both took a little step back from that corner. Old towers are funny things. I remembered an old photograph I'd seen of the north-west tower of St John's, Chester; whole one day, just fell in the night. Lucky there was no poor mason climbing the spiral stair at the time.

We took a thoughtful walk all round the parapet.

'Other three corners seem sound enough,' said Billy. 'An' a hell of a lot older. Claw-chisel marks on some of it.' He stamped on the stones beneath our feet, and made them ring with his hobnails. They sounded all right. No note like a cracked bell makes ...

'I'll go and have a word with Taff Evans,' I said. ''Sa bloody disgrace.'

'Here's Tommy Small wi' the pick-up. Hasn't he got another job at Ryland's this afternoon?'

'Aye, he'll be in a hurry. We'd best get the gear up, then. I'll see Taff when he's gone.'

We sent the sling of the hoist snaking down, and Tommy began fastening on the first load of scaffolding. He's a good reliable lad, for an apprentice. Just as well. We didn't want anything falling out of the sling. A nut-and-bolt falling from our height can smash a skull like a bullet smashes a pumpkin ...

'That stone's your responsibility,' I said. 'It's only at parapet level. It's not steeplejack's work.'

Taff Evans shifted his bum on the block of stone he

was sitting on in the sun, and stared at the remains of his ham sandwiches that lay beside him.

'It's just superficial damage,' he muttered. 'We'll get round to it. Always caused trouble, that bit round the gargoyle. No matter how you bed it. Main structure's sound enough . . .'

'If you don't watch it,' I said, 'that gargoyle will blow off one night, in a gale o' wind, and cause no end of damage. You wouldn't like it going through the nave roof . . .'

'That begger won't shift. Weighs a ton. Never has shifted, all the time I've been here. The architect knows about it . . .'

'Architect,' I snorted. 'What the hell does he know about it?' I've no time for architects, who come up top wi' their fancy two-hundred-guinea suits under their brand-new donkey jackets and hard hats. They don't work wi' stone; they work wi' sheets o' paper. They understand paper and money an' that's all.

Anyway, I went off in a bit of a rage, and had to let meself cool down before we started hammering wedges into the stone steeple to take our ladders. The wedges went in all right, and yet there was an odd little sound in the middle of the ringing of the hammer. A bit like . . . you'll think I'm mad, but it sounded to me a bit like a little kid crying out in pain, a little kid lost and frightened. It wasn't a sound I'd ever heard before, in stone or brick. It got to me so much, I actually went so far as to knock one of the wedges out again, to see how firm a hold it had. It was in very very firm indeed. I had to belt it sideways so hard it got away from me, and I watched in horror as it went twisting down through space, getting smaller and smaller. My heart was in my mouth, I can tell you. It coulda been a death. But it struck the wooden walkway inside the parapet of the nave, and there were only a few splinters of wood flying.

'Christ, Joe!' said Billy looking up at me, very pale. 'Steady on, will you?'

'Sorry. Won't happen again.'

'Bloody well hope not. We don't want this turning into one of *them* jobs . . .'

We both knew what he meant. The jobs when nothing goes right, no matter how careful you are. The jobs that try to kill somebody.

You do get them; we'd both had them.

Still, we made a nice job of the laddering-up. Of course, the ladders will always vibrate at the end of their iron stays. But that doesn't bother you, unless you lose your nerve and get the shakes and just stand there juddering the metal. Had a mate once who lost his nerve up there; took me three hours to get him down. Crying like a baby, he was – had to stay below him and nigh cuddle him, all the way down. He had to buy a bungalow, after that. Couldn't even stand a flight of stairs. Once your nerve's gone, it's gone.

But if you keep your nerve it's great up there, in your little nest of scaffold and planks at the top of the spire, just below the weather-vane. Two levels of planks, one to give you access to the weathercock, and one for your mate when you lift the much heavier weather-vane out of its socket – the thing marking north, south, east and west, that the weathercock turns on. We give ourselves handrails and all, of course – snug as a bug in a rug.

Course, once you're up at that height, you have to keep an eye on the clouds. Just as John Constable the painter had to, when he was a miller's son. That's why he came to paint clouds so well, they reckon. Bad weather, not spotted in time, could ruin a miller, make his mill run so fast it caught fire or blew to bits. That's our enemy, too. Not rain, but wind. A sudden squall, out of nowhere without warning, can tear you off the ladders. Rain – it doesn't matter, though it's not pleasant. Makes the stone slippery, especially where there's been pigeons roosting. That's why I wear hobnails, where some young fools wear trainers – trainers won't save you if you step in a pool of pigeon-shit, whereas hobnails is always the same.

You're in a different world up there. You hear what the wind brings you. If there's no wind, you might hear, faint and far off, the choir at evensong. Very sweet, though I can't see how they help some folk believe in God. They'd sound just as sweet singing dirty songs. Then a breeze comes, and the choir's gone, and you can hear the cows mooing in a field a mile away. That's even sweeter music to me – I'm a country boy at heart. After a week working in the smoke of the town, it's nice to get back to the country.

You don't get a lot of butterflies at that height; but towards dusk, you're on the same level as the swifts hunting insects. Screaming fit to deafen you, and whizzing past the back of your neck so you can feel the draught of them passing. Never come to earth, swifts, except to lay their eggs and raise their young. Ugly dark things, close-to. Devil-birds, us country lads used to call them.

We got the old weathercock out of its socket that night, so the lads could be setting it to rights in the workshop, while we were working on the spire. The spike it turned on was corroded and rough – bit of smoothing, good whack o' grease would see it right. I looked forward to putting it back regilded – a proud thing. When you see a weathercock shining bright gold in the sun, you know there's a church and a steeplejack that's on top of their affairs. Billy took it all the way down in a rope-sling on his back. It was heavy, but he wanted to do it that way. If we'd let it down on a rope we'd have risked damaging it. We like to carry everything up and down ourselves. When something you're lifting on the end of a rope hits against the building by accident, that's an ugly sound and has an ugly feel to it. That weathercock was a good piece of workmanship – three hundred years old and very simple – the body and the head round and solid, the rest cut from the flat plate. I don't care nowt for all this architects' prattling on about Gothic and Early English, but I respect a bit of good craftsmanship.

I was tidying up my things, preparatory to following Billy down for the night when I heard feet on the ladders and I thought, 'Hallo, what's he come back for?' Except the sound's wrong – the feet's too light for Billy.

Afore I can look to see who it is, a voice calls, 'Hallo Dad,' and our Kevin's face comes into view; grinning like a Cheshire cat. 'Mum's come,' he says. 'She's goin' to buy me some new trainers. She wants some shopping money.'

'Doesn't she always?' I say, and grin back at him, cos I'm proud of him.

But it's not much of a grin that night. Because I suddenly realize very much that I don't want him there. Not on that site. If it had've been some old chimney, I might have sat and talked with him on top for a bit, making the most of the sunshine, and yarning about his granda's days.

But I suddenly wanted him off that old steeple more than anything else in the world.

'Run down and tell yer Mam I'm just coming,' I says to him, calm and easy as I could.

Then I followed him down, quick as I could.

But he was younger and quicker, and reached the parapet ahead o' me. And I found him doing the very thing I didn't want to find him doing.

Staring at that bloody gargoyle, sitting in its bed of rotting stone. And the damned thing's sitting staring back, with its lichen-mottled face and blind, hollow eyes.

Now they were in the same world; now they knew each other, and I'd a given anything not to have it so.

'C'mon, Kevin,' I said joking. 'Get down them bloody stairs. You afraid of the dark or something?'

He didn't even answer me; he was that busy staring at the bloody thing, like a rabbit stares at the stoat that's going to kill it.

'Get on with yer, Kevin,' I said, giving him a push towards the little wooden door of the spiral staircase.

He seemed to come out of a day-dream. 'OK, Dad.'

That night, after we'd had our tea, Kevin and I went bird-watching. Not the usual sort, plodding round the fields with great binoculars round your neck (though I did take my work binoculars). No, we go up in the big trees in the wood, where the birds live. Right to the tops we go, where the branches sway and swing like a comfy bed, and you can look along the green billows of the tree-tops. In spring, we take the eggs out of the nests, handling them gentle, like, and putting them back afterwards of course. An' getting away quickly, so the hen-bird can come back and sit on them again. That's a wonder of life to me, to hold a speckled egg in the palm of your hand, and think what a marvellous thing it's going to become, a bird that flies and feeds and takes its chance with the cats, and breeds its own young and dies back into the dust in the end. Why does anyone need those crazy Christian dreams of Heaven, wi' angels playin' their harps on fleecy clouds, when they can have a wood at sunset, when you can look down from a low branch and see young rabbits playing, or even young foxes tumbling over and over and squeaking when they nip each other with their sharp little teeth?

Up there, Kevin an' I get real close to each other, as my dad and me did long before he was born. I'm that proud to teach him them same things, which egg belongs to which bird. And I'm that proud of him, the safe careful way he climbs, as fearless of heights as a cat. Even a full-grown horse-chestnut is no more to him than playing hopscotch on a pavement. I'd think what a grand steeplejack he'd make, when I'm gone, teaching his son an' grandson the same good old things.

And he's a different lad when he's up there; you get none of that stroppiness you get when his little mates are around and he's inclined to play up his mam, just like lads always do. We sit on some high branch, in the green shade, and we talk.

Only tonight, to spoil everything, he wanted to talk about that bloody gargoyle.

'What *are* gargoyles, Dad?' He swung his feet and looked at me expectantly.

'Waterspouts,' I said shortly. 'They throw the rain-water from the roof well clear, so it doesn't rot the foundations of the walls. Just old waterspouts.'

'Well . . . why do they carve them like that?'

'Well, they're just a bit of fun, like. Reckon the old masons got pretty bored, just carving bits of window-sill, or squaring up blocks of stone all day. One or two in every masons' gang must have been real artists, like sculptors are today. So when they got the chance, when work was slack and there wasn't no hurry, they'd carve a gargoyle for a bit of fun. There's one on Hapsham tower that's the spitting image of a stingy vicar, who wouldn't give the masons any beer-money when they'd done well. They carved his face real ugly, and his little hand holding his bag o' money tight, and they put him up on his own church tower, and showed him, and he never even recognized himself.'

He laughed then, the loveliest sound in the world to me, a sound as pretty as a bird's song, of pure joy. Then he went solemn again, and said, 'But they weren't all of stingy vicars?'

'No, son. Some reckoned they were made so ugly to frighten real devils away from the church. That's when people believed in devils, not like now. But most o' them . . . just the masons getting their own back, against the powers that be. People were very downtrodden

24

then, even masons, though masons were always a proud, bloody-minded lot.'

I wished I hadn't said all that to him, afterwards. It made me think of the old masons' gangs, that roamed the country quarrying their own stone and building churches. Funny old lot they were, living too close to each other, the master mason and the time-served journeymen, and the boy apprentices, living close on the road, without their womenfolk all summer, and their damned pride because they were the best, and their damned secrecy and odd beliefs. And the jealousy ... there's a church up in Scotland got something called the Prentice Pillar. The most marvellous bit of stone-carving you ever did see. Carved by a genius of an apprentice while his master was away. And when the master got back, he was seized with such jealousy he took a big hammer and smashed the lad's skull in like an egg.

You may think modern Freemasons are an odd lot, with their secret oaths and little aprons; but they are nothing to what the old masons were like.

That night, I wakened up screaming, sitting up soaked wi' sweat. I think I frightened our Barbara out of her wits.

'Joe, Joe,' she gabbled, grabbing me like she was trying to strangle me. 'What's the matter, whatever's the matter? Are you ill?'

'Just a dream,' I said slowly, so as not to frighten her. 'Just a stupid old dream.' I think I said it more to comfort myself, for I never usually dream at all, and this one was bloody slow to fade.

'That's not like you,' she said. 'It's not like you at all. You're in a muck-sweat. I'll have to get you a change of pyjamas. You've got the sheets soaked an' all. And my nightie. Look.' She switched the light on. 'What were you dreaming about?'

'Work,' I said, raising my eyebrows and forcing a half-grin and trying to make a joke of it for her sake.

'You're not losing your nerve, are you? Your head for heights?'

That made me angry, which helped. 'Don't talk wet, woman. I'm a *Clarke*.' And it's true. I wasn't losing my nerve or my head for heights. It was nothing about that.

Anyway, I changed my pyjamas, after towelling myself down. And lay back down again, but not to sleep. I didn't sleep a wink till it was time to get up, just lay and held her and listened to her breathing.

And thinking about that dream. Which was why I didn't dare go back to sleep again.

Cos I dreamt that I was standing in the dark, looking up at the south-west tower of Muncaster cathedral. And our Kevin was up there on top, in the dark, and screaming as if some wild beast was eating him. And the door to the tower was locked and I didn't have the key. I remember that I was so desperate that I tried to climb up the outside of the tower, up the buttress. But I knew I'd never get there in time to save Kevin. And when I was less than half-way up, the tower began to crack open in front of my very eyes ...

Which is why I wakened up screaming.

The next morning, I felt dog-rough. Rougher than I'd ever felt in my life. That dream was inside my brain, and I couldn't get it out. It kept coming back and making me do stupid things, like putting jam on my toast before I'd put any butter on.

I knew I shouldn't go up that day. It wasn't that I was scared; I felt too dull and weary to be scared for myself. But I owed it to Billy. And to Barbara, and young Kevin. Better to lose a day's work than to ...

Anyway, it was raining; pissing down whole rods. I rang up Billy and gave him a fiddling list of little jobs to do round the workshops, things so unimportant they'd been waiting for months. And then I drove down to the cathedral ...

Then I went up an' faced the gargoyle. It looked an even uglier bugger in the rain. The rotten stone that I'd crumbled away with my finger-nail yesterday had dissolved into yellow puddles.

I looked at the gargoyle, and I said to it, 'I'll settle your bloody hash, you see if I don't.' Then I laid a spare plank across the parapet at that corner, to fence it off, like you might pen up a mad bull.

That made me feel better at first; then I realized I was talking out loud to the bloody thing, and that made me feel worse, as if it had won the first round.

So I went down to take it out on Taffy Evans, who hadn't a lot to do either, in the rain. He's a hard man to have a row with, Taffy Evans. Not a typical Welshman, cos he's fair, flaxen-haired, while most of them are dark. And he's tall and thin, where a lot of them are small. And he's got a long head, and a long nose with gold-rimmed spectacles, where most Welshmen I've met are round-headed, with little snub noses. I reckon one of his ancestors must have been a raping, pillaging

Saxon. He's got the Welsh Nonconformist stubborn-
ness though; always in the right is Taffy, and he'll
argue all day to prove it. Chapel preacher, Bible-
puncher, which is funny in the foreman-mason of an
Anglican cathedral.

To be fair to him, I don't think he wanted a row
that morning. He was miserable with the rain and the
idleness, and just wanted to be left alone to brood. But
I laced straight into him, in front of his lads, about the
state of that stone round the gargoyle. He took it for a
long time, just saying yes and no, and then he said
finally,

'You got your work schedule?'

'Yeah.'

'What does it say?'

'Renovate the weather-vane an' weathercock. Cut out
and replace substandard stone blocks in the steeple.'

'Why don't you just go and do it then? And mind
your own business, boyo.' His voice always got very
Welsh when he got mad.

'That stone's ...'

'What do you know about stone? You're only a
flipping steeplejack. We even have to saw your stone
blocks for you. Jack of all trades and master of none.'

'You try hanging from a rope-sling two hundred feet
up ...'

His lads were gathering round us in a circle. Pretty
hostile circle too. Always stick together, masons ... it
could've got pretty nasty, if the phone extension in the
mason's yard hadn't rung just then. Very proud of their
new telephones, the cathedral. Maybe they're hoping
the Almighty will give them a bell one day ...

'For you,' said Taffy, shoving it towards my ear so hard he almost brained me.

It was Billy. 'Your missus said you'd gone down to the cathedral . . .'

'Well?'

'I've been on the phone to me Uncle Jim. About when he last replaced the stone around that gargoyle.'

'You're supposed to be *workin*'!'

'Done all the jobs you gave me. Didn't take an hour. Well, do you want to know what he said, or don't you?'

'Go on, then!'

'Said he replaced that stone in 1971.'

'Twenty years ago? For heck's sake, what stone did he use? Stuff from his rockery at home?'

'Best Kerridge. He said he chose the best very careful; because the last lot had rotted since *1951*.'

'Bloody hell. What else did he say?'

'Only that there was a nasty smell while they was working. Even the wind didn't seem to blow it away. There was lots of jokes about farting an' dead rats . . . funny thing for him to remember, after all that time . . .'

'Right, thanks.' I tried to think of more jobs for him to be getting on with, but my mind wasn't on it, so I hung up, afore I made a fool of myself in front of all them masons, who were starting to snigger among themselves.

I turned back to Taffy Evans. 'Replaced in 1971 and 1951 afore that.' He knew what I'd been talking about.

'So what?' he said. '*Our* business. Why are you gettin' your knickers in a twist?' That got another snigger. I felt like hitting him. But I just said, 'What happens to the old job-books?' I knew they kept records of what work they had to do, when it was done, and when it was signed off.

'We hand them on to the museum. Go and bother *her* for a change . . .'

I went, to further sniggers. I knew where the new museum was, in the cloisters, because our Kevin had been there with his class from school. He'd said the lady in charge was very nice and friendly.

They'd spent a lot of money in the cloisters, to attract what tourists came to Muncaster. A restaurant where they served home-made soup and home-baked scones, and the museum, which is really a lot of high-security glass cases in pitch-darkness, only lit by little spotlights shining on the cathedral's silver and gold. Not what I call a museum; I like to see what I'm doing, not blundering around in the dark. It was so dark I had bother finding the curator, and I had to explain what I wanted in the dark, without being able to see her face. I felt a *proper* fool.

But she was a nice woman, like our Kevin had said. She took me into her office, where there was still some daylight, and bent and produced a pile of old job-books from the bottom of a cupboard, and let me use her desk to look at them. It took me three hours, because every fiddling job they do is entered up, even repairing the Dean's front doorstep. But I got on the trail of what I wanted in the end, by jumping back every twenty years or so.

That stonework had been repaired every twenty years, roughly, going back to when the first job-book started in 1846 . . .

But what made me really twitch were the delays, also recorded.

'Work held up by broken pulley . . .'

'Scaffolding blew down in high wind on 17/3/32 . . .'

'A. Smith taken to hospital . . .'

Every time, it seemed, it was *that* sort of job.

The Curator kept popping in, to see how I was getting on, the way they do. And she must have spotted my mood. As I said, she was a nice woman, sympathetic. Hair done up tight in a bun, but her blue eyes behind her spectacles were full of concern. I wondered why no one had married her.

'Something's worrying you, Mr Clarke?'

'Something funny about the south-west tower . . .' I said, feeling uncomfortable, not wanting to sound a fool.

'Now there *is* something odd about the south-west tower. I should be able to remember but . . .' She twisted her smooth high forehead into a terrible frown. I wished she wouldn't do that; the creases might get permanent, and she was only quite young . . .

Then the office door opened again. Her face cleared.

'Here's the Reverend Morris. He's bound to know.' Her voice implied that the Reverend Morris was God, or something very similar.

I went all tight, inside. I'd heard of the Reverend Morris. One of the bishop's two chaplains. The Reverend Morris, who was always getting himself into the local paper, more often than Paddy Ferguson the town drunk. The Reverend Morris who believed in brighter services, like dancing in the aisles and waving your hands in the air, and people in the congregation babbling gibberish in the middle of the sermon, and asking people if they were *saved*. One of *them*. There seem to be more and more of them, every month that passes.

'Mr Clarke, isn't it? How can I help you, Mr Clarke?' He put a large heavy pudgy hand on my shoulder, like he owned me. He sounded like he knew more about me than I knew about myself. I had to stop myself giving a wriggle to shake his hand off. I can't stand fellers touching me who I hardly know, though I don't mind women doing it.

'I'm making enquiries about the south-west tower,' I said, stiffly as a policeman in a magistrate's court.

'Ah, yes, the south-west tower. Very interesting, the south-west tower.' He was instantly certain he knew all about the bloody thing, like he would always pretend he knew everything about everything. 'Let's take a little walk, Mr Clarke. Far better if you see it with your own eyes.'

And he bore me off towards the door, hand still on my shoulder. I felt I was under some sort of holy arrest. He marched me all the way through the cloisters, across both transepts and out into the rain of the cathedral green, still with his hand lovingly on my shoulder.

'Are you a Christian, Mr Clarke?' I'd known the question wouldn't be long in coming. He asks everybody, they tell me, before he's hardly been introduced. Now I don't know *what* I am really. When I look at our Kevin laughing, or at our cat playing with its tail, I wonder if there is a God, because they're both grand things, and somebody must've made them. On the other hand, I read all the terrible things in the papers and I think that if there is a God, he must have lost interest and pushed off to mend some different universe.

I suppose my mind's open, really. But the way this feller went on, with his warm over-familiar squishy ways, you just wanted to build as big a wall as possible between him and you, as quick as possible.

So I said, 'No, I'm a militant atheist.'

At least his hand dropped off my shoulder, pronto. He said, in a hurt voice,

'It seems odd, a militant atheist working on the House of God.'

'What's it matter, providing the rain's kept out? We do a first-class job ...'

'Oh, I'm sure, I'm sure. Anyway, here we have it, the south-west tower. Look at it closely, Mr Clarke; then look at the north-west tower. *Really* closely. Don't you *notice* something? Something different?'

Now if there's one thing I can't stand, even more than blokes who put their hand on your shoulder, or blokes who dance in the aisle, it's blokes who play guessy-games with you, in gloaty but-surely-you-can-see-it voices. It makes me feel about an inch high, it makes my head whirl so I can't notice *anything*. Which is the effect that they want, I suppose.

'Look the same to me,' I said. I wanted to hit him.

'Look again, *really* closely.'

Gritting my teeth, I made myself look really closely. Finally I said, sure it had nothing to do with it,

'The window arches are more pointed on the north-west tower.'

'Got it in one, Mr Clarke. Got it in one.'

The patronizing sod.

'And what does that *mean*, Mr Clarke?'

'Buggered if I know,' I said. That made him flinch, I can tell you. But it seemed to get through even his elephantine hide that he wasn't doing himself any good.

'It means the south-west tower was built nearly three hundred years after the north-west. The Normans built both towers up to roof-top level, and then they ran out of money and stopped – it happened all over the country.'

'Over-ambitious,' I said. 'Like the Channel Tunnel rail-link.'

'Not at all, not at all. They built with faith, to the glory of God. They knew God would supply the money to finish them, in His own good time.'

'Three hundred years,' I said. 'I hope none of the masons starved to death.'

'Oh, no. They would go on to other work, elsewhere. They went from place to place . . .'

'I know that,' I said. 'I was making a joke.'

He gave me a funny look. He might know about dancing in the aisles, but he couldn't recognize a joke when he heard one. I've heard since those Characteristic Fundamentalists are all the same. No real sense of humour.

'Then they finished the north-west tower in 1257, but they had to wait till 1538 for the other one . . .'

'Why was that?'

That had him; he hadn't a clue. I wondered if he'd cover up with a flood of that speaking-in-tongues gibberish they do. But he just said,

'I don't know, but I will find out. That's what they taught us to say in the Army, when I was an officer-

34

cadet, you know.' He said, 'Good day to you, Mr Clarke,' and stalked away. He had a big bottom and it wobbled under the tails of his sports coat as he walked. I can't stand men with big wobbly bottoms. I wondered how much it would wobble when he was dancing in the aisles. I was glad he was only in charge of God, and not the Army's nuclear artillery.

I spent a bit of time hanging around the cathedral green, looking up at that tower. I felt a bit better. It wasn't just me, then. There *was* something funny about the thing, something nobody wanted to talk about. Maybe my dream was just a warning that there was something wrong with the tower: some steeplejack's instinct that I couldn't plumb. Something in the stone. Then I went home to have a shower and put my feet up, and help our Kevin with his homework on the home life of the hedgehog.

The next day was fine-ish, just a bit of drizzle, and we went back to work. I was glad of the drizzle. It meant we didn't take our lunch-break on top of the tower; we had it in a caff in town. I didn't fancy eating my sarnies with that thing for company, even though I hadn't had any more bad dreams.

I spent the day in a rope-cradle, which was let down from the tip of the steeple. First, in the morning, I marked the rotten blocks of stone in the steeple with yellow chalk. There weren't a lot of them, and they were just suffering from ordinary weathering. It wouldn't be a long job, thank God. Then, in the afternoon, I began cutting them away with a chisel. Knocked most of the stone out with a point, then smoothed the bottom of the hole with a claw-chisel, ready to take the cement that would hold the new block in place. I measured each block, so that the masons could cut me new ones with their stone-saw. No two blocks were quite the same size; no two seemed to be carved by the same man. The steeple was a patchwork of men's hands, five hundred years old. Some blocks were Victorian or later, cut with the stone-saw. But a lot were earlier, Georgian, medieval. The marks every mason had made with his chisel were different, like fingerprints; no mason has the same style exactly, and the claw-marks on a lot of them were still quite clear, in spite of the weathering. Here was a steady bloke, getting on neat and workmanlike with his job. Here was a real flashy show-off, every claw-mark beautifully lined up, a perfectionist. Here was some poor apprentice, claw-marks going sloppy; all over the place, then suddenly smartening up. Probably the master mason caught him day-dreaming and gave him a good clout over the ear. Funny how real the work of men's hands is; I felt very close to them; journeymen, apprentices, gaffer. I thought you lot could tell me a thing or two about what happened wi' that gargoyle, if you were still around. One of you buggers knows. Or more than one . . .

There was a yell from up top, on the platform. Billy.

'Joe, I'm outa fags. OK to nip across to the shop?'

Bloody Billy out of fags again. Not content with raining empty packets and even lighted dog-ends down on top of me, he *would* run out of fags.

Something warned me not to let him go from up top, while I was dangling there. If anything went wrong . . .

On the other hand, the shop was just across the cathedral green. Five minutes there, five minutes back (Billy was young and fitter than me), and he was unbearable without his fags, got real ratty. And the sky was clear by then. What could go wrong?

'OK.'

I heard his feet go clanging down the ladder on the far side of the spire, and went on cutting out the rotten block of stone. Then I finished, cleared out the chippings and dust in a tiny shower, and went to move on to the next block.

The rope would not move in my hands.

Somewhere up top, something had seized up; maybe the rope had come off a pulley.

I hung, quite helpless. Ten feet from the top platform; ninety feet from the parapet below, two hundred feet to the ground ...

Nothing to worry about, of course. As long as the ropes held. As long as there wasn't some sharp metallic edge up there, chewing away at one of them.

Billy wouldn't be long. Once he was back, it would be easy enough. Take it easy, I told myself. Take a break. Enjoy the view.

After several looks at the view, I glanced at my watch. The beggar had been gone nearly twenty minutes; there was no sign of him crossing the green, prominent in his spotless white T-shirt and faded denims. Christ, I'd give him what for when he came back. But there was no need to panic ...

When half an hour had passed, my bum began to ache, from sitting so terribly still in the cradle. When you're moving about you don't notice the way it cuts into you. Where the hell had he got to . . .?

Clouds coming up from the west. Big nasty clouds. Be half an hour before they got here, but when they did, we were going to get very wet; there were scarves of dark rain hanging under the clouds already.

It must be ten years since anything as stupid as this had happened to me.

That bloody gargoyle; the list of accidents on the south-west tower I'd read up in the old job-books yesterday . . .

I looked down at the gargoyle, and it looked back at me.

I felt like a mouse in the paw of a cat. *And* a mouse that was going to get thoroughly pissed on. Or worse.

It wasn't the height that was bugging me; it was the having to sit still. I began trying to work out crazy ways of getting back up to the platform, or down to the parapet. Crazy, crazy ways that broke all the rules . . . hand over hand up the ropes . . . crazy, crazy. But the having to sit there was driving me crazy. People watching me from the ground. But if I shouted, my voice wouldn't carry. If I waved, they would merely wave back. The clouds' shadow fell across the spire. I could almost hear the rain coming, the air was magnifying every sound to four times its normal volume . . .

It suddenly struck me that something serious might have happened to Billy; he might have been knocked down in the street by a car, coming out of the shop. He was a bit of a dreamer, a bit dozy at ground level, though never when he was high up.

And if he got knocked down, taken to hospital, killed even, they wouldn't know who he was or where he'd come from. He'd carry no ID, just money. I could dangle here for the rest of the day, till it got dark. Barbara wouldn't even start to worry about me till it got dark. And even then the last place they'd think of looking for me was up the spire ... I could still be here in the morning, helpless, soaked and soaked again. And that was if the bloody rope that was holding me didn't give way ... by the morning, I'd be a raving nut-case and a physical wreck into the bargain.

You understand, I still wasn't scared of heights; that was the last thing I was scared of. But to be helpless. I seriously began considering getting myself out of that sling, and shinning up the ropes hand over hand. The platform was only ten feet above me; I'd make it easily. It was very tempting.

Unless something else went wrong. Like the blocked pulley coming loose when I was half-way up; or the rope giving way with the extra heaves I would be putting on it. I thought again about the accidents in the old job-books. Maybe *they* weren't really accidents either.

Perhaps the gargoyle, the tower, was really trying to ...? No, I said, no. I'll not budge from this sling, if it kills me. I unfastened the rope and then tied it extra tight.

The next ten minutes were the longest of my life. And then there was a clanging on the ladder; Billy was back, and I felt a right idiot for my fears.

His stupid, *stupid* face peered down.

'Hey, Joe, you stuck? Won't be a minute. Try *that*.'

With hands that absurdly wouldn't stop shaking, I got myself out of the mess.

'Where the hell you *been*? You said ten minutes!'

'Met that vicar mate of yours in the shop. That Morris. Least he reckoned he was a big mate of yours. All over me he was.' Billy wriggled his brawny T-shirt-covered shoulders uncomfortably; I knew how he was feeling. 'He said he had something for you, back in his office. Something you'd want more than a pint o' lager. He was so persistent I went back with him for it. Then he began going on about was I a *Christian*? I couldn't get away from him.'

His face was such a study, I couldn't help forgiving him. There was never any harm in Billy; just too easily led. I laughed, and it helped.

'What you got for me, then?'

'Oh, yeah.' He reached into the back pocket of his jeans and produced a folded, very bent piece of paper that looked like a photocopy.

I unfolded it; it was. A photocopy from some old book; a crude engraving of the west end of Muncaster cathedral, with a pair of pointed towers. The only snag was that one of them, the south-west tower, was busy falling down, in a most spectacular way. I mean, not only was the tower falling down, but heavy, bulging clouds filled the sky, and they were stitched together with jagged bits of lightning. Lots of little people were standing pointing, or running away, and there were houses and they were all old half-timbered things. Three separate bits of lightning were hitting the tower, and the label underneath said,

'The fall of the south-west tower, 1257'.

Billy looked over my shoulder. 'That's cheering. I hope they got it right second time round.'

'So do I. Let's jack it in for the rest of the day.'

We just got down the ladder before the heavy rain really started. I was wondering if somebody was really trying to kill me, and who it was. The tower, or the Reverend Mr Morris. Or both.

I had the dream again, that night. Our Kevin screaming on top of the tower, and the tower door locked.

But I didn't wake up screaming. Barbara wakened me up, tugging frantically at my shoulder.

'Joe. I looked in on Kevin. He's not in his bed.'

Barbara's the restless one in our family; up once or twice to the loo every night, or she's not happy. Kevin and me always sleep right through, like logs. All my family do.

'Gone to the loo?' I asked dopily, trying to get the dream out of my head.

'I've just been to the loo, stupid. He's not there.'

'Gone down to the kitchen, to grab a cheese butty?' Our Kevin likes to carve himself a cheese butty when nobody's looking. Cheese half an inch thick, and bread double that. Then he eats half of it and chucks the rest under his bed till later. Barbara finds the fossilized remains when she cleans his room at the end of the week; thick with dust. Good pull-in for mice, our Kevin's room.

'Joe, I've checked everywhere. He's nowhere in the house. And the front door's wide open ...'

I said something unprintable, and whacked out of bed stark naked. Ran through and felt Kevin's bed. It was stone-cold. He'd been gone a bit.

And his clothes were still lying where Barbara had

picked them up and folded them neatly on to a chair.

'He's in his bloody pyjamas.' You have to come to blows with Kevin to get him to change out of his usual T-shirt and jeans, even to go to his granny's for Sunday afternoon tea.

'Joe, he must be walking in his sleep.'

'Don't be daft, woman. Our Kevin's never walked in his sleep. None of our family have ever walked in their sleep.'

'Well, where is he? Why don't you do something, 'stead of standing there arguin'?'

The clock on the dining-room mantelpiece suddenly struck three.

'He could've been gone for hours. Where's he *gone*?'

I thought wildly. With a three-hour or four-hour start, he could've been anywhere. Except ... and it hit me like a bolt of lightning ... there was one place I was afraid of, beyond all others.

The south-west tower.

Suddenly, I didn't care if he was lying in some ditch, or lost in some wood. He'd meet nowt worse there than a fox or a badger. I ran upstairs and shoved on a sweater and a pair of jeans.

'Where you goin', Joe? You can't *leave* me wi' this.'

'Ring the bloody police, Barbara. Ring round the neighbours.' But don't stop me.

I was running down the stairs and out to the van. I didn't care where he was, if he wasn't at that tower.

It's seven miles from where we live to Muncaster. I did the first five in about four minutes; thank God the road was empty.

And then, after five miles, I saw something pale lying

on the road, shining up in the headlights. I got out, and picked it up. But I knew what it was, before I picked it up.

Kevin's pale blue striped pyjama trousers.

I pulled up in Cathedral Close. There wasn't a thing moving, bar a solitary black and white cat. I ran to the tower door. I'd locked it when we finished work, and taken the key back to Taffy Evans.

But now the door opened to a touch.

'Kevin?' I bellowed up the spiral stair. 'Kevin?' There was no reply. I started up like all the hounds of hell were after me. My panting breath filled the narrow spiral up through the stone, and echoed, as if the tower itself was breathing.

On to the parapet in the moonlight. No sign of Kevin.

But the gargoyle stared at me, its hollow eyes full of shadow.

'If you've harmed him,' I shouted, 'I'll do for you. Slow. Wi' a claw-chisel. There'll be nowt left of you they can't use as road-chippings.'

It just went on staring at me.

'Kevin,' I bawled. 'Kevin?'

Was that something fluttering, something white, on the top platform on the spire?

Up I went, wi' only thin trainers on. The rungs of the ladder bit into my feet something cruel.

I reached the top. No Kevin. The white fluttering thing was an old piece of rag that Billy must've tied on to the handrail to keep it handy.

Suddenly I was scared stiff. Had Kevin come up here

43

and fallen? I looked down, terrified of seeing a tiny, still, sprawling figure on top of the nave roof or on the grass by the west door. But at that moment, the moon went behind a cloud, and there was pitch darkness. I could see nothing.

'Kevin,' I yelled, hanging on to the handrail with slippery hands and nearly overbalancing in my panic. 'KEVIN?'

As if in answer to my yells, a car came round the corner into Cathedral Close. A police car with a revolving blue light on the roof. It pulled up at the very door of the tower. A policeman got out; I could just see his bulky foreshortened shape in the flashing of the revolving blue light.

I despaired then. Policemen came to tell you when somebody you loved had had an accident. They came to tell us when I was a kid, and my grandma got knocked down and killed by a lorry on the Whitegate Road. I clung to the rail with both hands, wi' my eyes shut, to stop me throwing myself over. Barbara will need you, I kept telling myself. Barbara will need you.

I might have hung there for ever, if a carefully calm shout hadn't come from the parapet.

'What you doin' up there, sunshine?' Then, 'Would you mind coming down careful-like, sunshine? I'd like a little word with you.'

It wasn't the way anyone talks to a bereaved father. It was the way people talk to a crazy drunk, or a potential suicide. It gave me hope. I got hold of myself and got myself down the iron ladder.

The fuzz took a very firm grip of my arms.

'Now, lad, what you on, then?'

'It's all right,' I said, 'you can let go of me. I'm all right. I'm the steeplejack working here.'

They looked at me with disbelieving eyes.

'Working overtime?' said the bigger one. 'Or is it the night shift?' I saw myself as they must see me, jeans and a sweater, and bare feet in trainers, tousled hair.

The smaller one sniffed my breath. 'He's not been drinking. Drugs, you reckon?'

'Look,' I said, 'I'm sorry to have caused any bother . . .'

'Any bother?' said the bigger one. 'Shouting your head off up the steeple in the middle of the night? You've got the whole of Cathedral Close aroused. The Dean phoned us his-self . . .'

'Beginner's Night, this,' said his mate. 'First that kid near stark naked, then this nutter . . .'

'What kid?' I shouted, my heart swelling big as a football.

'Kid in only a pyjama top, walking across the close here an hour ago. We nearly knocked him down. Stepped right out in front of us. Reckon he was sleep-walking. Couldn't get a word of sense out of him. Took him to Muncaster General.'

'Lad about eight, blond hair?' I shouted, wild with hope.

'Yeah, about that.'

'I'm his dad. I was looking for him, up the tower. Shouting his name.'

They looked at each other, doubtfully. Then the big one said, still full of suspicion, 'We'll run you to the hospital. You can give us a few names and addresses while we're going.'

It was an Indian doctor I talked to. A Doctor Kumar; nice bloke, half-worried, half-fascinated.

'A strange case. We have examined him physically. He has come to no harm, though his feet are cut and bleeding. But he is in some sort of ... mental state. He does not see when I hold up two fingers in front of him. He will not answer questions. And three times he has tried to get out of bed and escape from the hospital – the sister just caught him as he was leaving, the first time. Now we are watching him all the time. You say he walked from Joynton? With bare feet? Just like we found him?'

'Yeah,' I said. 'Can I see him? Can I ring my wife? She'll be frantic.'

'Yes to both of those things, Mr Clarke. If you will come with me ...'

'He's all right,' I told Barbara. 'He's in Muncaster General. Don't drive in till you've calmed yourself down.'

'Marge is with me. She'll drive me in. Is he ... hurt?'

'Only his feet, bleeding.' I didn't want to upset her more, till she got there.

Our Kevin lay on his back, in a little side ward with only two beds, and the other one empty. A bloke in a coat that I took to be a hospital porter was sitting by his bedside. He got up as we came in.

'He's quieter now, Doctor.'

'We have given him a strong sedative,' said Dr Kumar.

'He's been talking again, though. Can't make head nor tail of it . . .'

I bent over Kevin. He looked angelic, with his face washed and his hair brushed. I shook him gently by the shoulder.

'Kevin, Kevin, it's Dad. Dad's here, you're all right now.'

'I don't think he can hear you, Mr Clarke.'

'Wait,' I said. Kevin's eyes opened; then his lips parted, as if he wanted to say something.

But all that came out were long ugly words, that I couldn't understand, and that Kevin could never have said when he was himself.

'What you done to him? What you done to him?' I shouted.

Dr Kumar put a gentle hand on my arm. 'We have done nothing but give him a sedative. Come away, Mr Clarke, you will only distress yourself, and not help Kevin.'

'But what's he saying?'

'I do not know, Mr Clarke. But from my little experience of the classics, back at my Bombay school, I would say he is talking in Latin. Only a very strange kind of Latin.'

'But he doesn't know any Latin. They don't do it — only a bit of French . . .'

'That is what makes it so puzzling, Mr Clarke. But rest assured, he will get the very best possible care . . .'

Just then Barbara arrived, and I won't go into *that*.

The hospital staff were very good. They let us stay by

47

his bedside the rest of the night, if we were quiet. I dozed a bit, and so did Barbara beside me. It was the effects of shock, I reckon. You sleep, once you know the worst is over.

Barbara and I hung around that hospital all the next day. I had no thoughts of going to work; I rang Billy at the workshops and he was very sympathetic. I sent him with one of the other lads, whose mate was on holiday, to demolish a little chimney at Lippington. It was standing alone on the site; there was no chance of anything being buggered up; I reckoned they could manage on their own, for once. Billy was a sensible sort of lad.

At the hospital, they kept on taking Kevin away for tests, in case he'd suffered some accident while he was on the road to Muncaster. EEG, ECG, I don't know. But everything they did drew a blank. They couldn't find anything wrong with him. Except the moment they turned their backs, he'd start to try to get away from them, out of the hospital. They said it seemed to come on him in fits; I saw one of them start, while he was actually lying in bed. He made a flat dive for the window, without warning, and it was on the first floor and all. It was me that grabbed him; he fought like a devil, tried to bite me on the arm. Mumbling those strange ugly words. His eyes were open, but he didn't know me. I wasn't even a person to him; just an obstacle. I looked in his eyes, and it just wasn't our Kevin at all, but some mad thing. It near broke my heart. I couldn't believe it was happening to us. I couldn't touch a bite to eat, or even drink. They kept filling him up with sedatives, and talked about sending him to another hospital, a hospital for nutters.

At five o'clock, I had a call from Billy. The chimney was down safe; no sweat. He sounded cock-a-hoop. It was the first one he'd laid on his own. I said well done, but I couldn't have cared less.

When my mind wasn't on Kevin, it was on that tower. The tower was after our Kevin all right. If that police car hadn't have grabbed him by accident, he'd have gone up it. Beyond that, I couldn't think what might have happened; I couldn't bear to. I didn't say anything to our Barbara; she was going through enough without her thinking that *I'd* taken leave of my senses too. To her, I suppose, I'd just gone looking for our Kevin, and then rung up to say I'd found out where he was. She didn't get round to asking me any questions; but maybe she would, later. Well, cross that bridge when we come to it.

In between his fits, Kevin just lay as if he was asleep. I tried to read the paper a nurse had fetched me, but I couldn't make any sense of it; kept reading the same thing over and over again, in between going out into the corridor to stare at the fire hydrant.

It finally happened about midnight. I was dozing, I think, dozing over that stupid newspaper. Suddenly I heard our Kevin say,

'Mum? Dad? Where am I? What are we doing here?' He sounded muzzy, half-asleep, but it was our Kev all right. Our Kev come back. Barbara grabbed him and hugged him, and I went out to get the nurse and she fetched the doctor. When I got back in the room,

Barbara was just sitting on the bed and hugging him, with tears streaming down her face.

The nurse and doctor did all the usual things: pulse, temperature, shining a little pencil-torch first into Kevin's left eye, then his right. You could see they were totally baffled. But they made such a glad fuss, I knew they'd been *bloody* worried; they just hadn't shown us how worried they were.

Then Kevin started demanding something to eat and drink. They fetched him a mug of Ovaltine and some chocolate biscuits the nurse had bought for herself. They were that chuffed. Barbara was all for taking our Kevin home, but the doctor said they'd keep him in for a few days. And I agreed with him. Only *he* was going on about the delayed effects of shock and concussion. And *I* was thinking about that damned tower. Maybe the tower was just letting our Kevin go, for a bit, so we would drop our guard ...

Still, I slept that night, on a very uncomfortable couch in the corridor, while Barbara dozed on the spare bed in Kevin's ward. In the morning, Kevin wakened up his old self, bright as a button.

So I left them there, and went back to work at the cathedral, feeling dog-rough. Still, it was a nice cool bright morning, as Billy and I climbed our fixed ladders to the steeple; and I'd managed to shake most of the cobwebs away.

'We'd better get the weather-vane down first, Billy.' The weather-vane's not easy like the weathercock. It can be a right bastard. Its four arms, north, south, east and west, tend to catch on everything as you're lowering it to the ground, and it's quite a weight. Anyway, we got to it, and got it out of its stone socket, and were just working it out through the scaffolding when Billy says, suddenly, 'Jesus Christ, what's that?'

I felt him let go of the vane; the weight of the vane nearly broke my back, trying to tear itself out of my hands and down ... I couldn't hold it; it was pulling me after it.

I let go.

It flung itself loose like a bronze bird, dwindled away down the slope of the spire till it hit near the bottom. I saw the yellow scar grow in the black Keuper stone, saw the cloud of yellow stone-fragments fly. Saw the vane leap outwards towards the ring of spectators with upturned white faces who were standing on the grass of the cathedral green.

Just in time the ring of faces parted, scattered. With a thud that floated clear up to us, it embedded itself in the green turf.

I turned on Billy. 'You stupid bastard, you coulda *killed* somebody.'

But he wasn't looking at me. He was pointing with a shaking finger at something that lay behind the parapet of the nave roof, far below.

A tiny sprawled figure in pyjamas. It coulda been our Kevin, for its blond hair lifted in the morning breeze; the hair was the only thing moving in a splatter of blood that lay like splashed ink across the green lead of the nave roof.

It *couldn't* be our Kevin. I'd left him safe in hospital, eating his breakfast, and driven straight to the tower and started work. I'd have heard him come, seen him come ...

And the pyjamas were the wrong colour, a pretty forget-me-not blue, whereas I'd left our Kevin wearing washed-out grey hospital things with stripes . . .

It wasn't our Kevin, cos I helped the police and the undertakers get him down, when the police had finished poking around. But he was our Kev's age, and blond. They knew his name by that time, because his parents had reported him missing two hours previous; missing in the middle of the night in his pyjamas. His name was Tom Charnock, and he lived in a house in Cathedral Close, because he was the son, the only son, of one of the stipendiary canons of the cathedral.

I knew by then what had happened. I'd worked it out. Why the tower had let go of our Kevin. It had found another victim, a lot nearer.

I was questioned by a detective-sergeant called Hughie Allardyce. A tough cookie once, but getting fat and past it. There were stains on the lapels of his brown pin-striped suit, and egg on his tie. But he was still sharp, and nasty with it.

'All right,' he said, when I'd sat down. 'I've rung the hospital and you've got an alibi. At the relevant time, you were snoring in a hospital corridor with your mouth open, and nurses passing all the time. And the hospital's four miles from the cathedral, the buses had stopped running, and your car was hemmed into the car-park by the night staff's cars. Just as bloody well for you. But you've still got a few questions to answer, haven't you, *Mr* Clarke? Like what the hell the tower door was doing unlocked, and what you were doing up there the previous night, yelling your bloody head off and waking up the whole district?'

I shook my head, trying to clear it, and decided to answer the simpler question first.

'We locked up as usual two nights ago, after work. Took the key back to Taffy Evans. He'll tell you.'

'He told me you handed in the key. He didn't see you lock the door.'

'My mate Billy saw me lock the door. He was with me.'

'Aye, so he says. But mates stick together, tell the same story, don't they? Maybe you were in a hurry, careless. The door was unlocked when you got back to it, late that night. Or else how did you get in? Or have you got your own key?'

'What would I want with my own key? And I locked it, I tell you. I'm careful about things like that.'

'Don't get your knickers in a twist. The day after your goings-on had aroused the whole Close, the Dean went with Taffy Evans and saw to the door himself personally.'

I shook my head to clear it again. It wasn't making sense.

'So why was it unlocked again, the next night, so that poor little bugger Tom Charnock could get up there?' he said.

I could still only shake my head in bewilderment.

'Because there's a fault in the lock, Mr Clarke. It *seems* to lock, and then, after a couple of minutes, something gives inside, and it swings a bit open again. I've seen it happen.'

'So why bother me about it?'

'Well, there was no complaints about the door unlocking itself again before you went up there to see to the spire. Damage it, did you? Not let on, in case you had to pay for it?'

'Don't talk wet. I carry plenty of insurance ...'

'Maybe you wanted to keep your no-claims bonus? Anyway, I've had a locksmith to look at it. He says fair wear and tear.'

'So?'

'So you didn't notice it was going wrong – the lock? Not before the night you went up there looking for your lad ...'

'It was unlocked that night. But it was locked when we got there this morning ...'

We stared at each other.

'If it was locked this morning, how did the lad get up there last night? How *could* he have fallen off the tower?'

'It was locked all right this morning. Ask Billy.'

'Do you know what you're *saying*? If it was locked this morning, that's half-way to proof of a murder.'

'Aye,' I said, with deep feeling. 'Aye.'

'And I've been talking to your wife. I know what happened about your lad ...'

'That's all she needs, after what she's been through the last two days ...'

'We've got our job to do ... seems to me what happened to your lad is what happened to this Tommy Charnock. Exactly the same. Sleep-walking in the middle of the night. Or snatched from his bed. Found by the cathedral. Your lad was heading for the door of the south-west tower when my lads picked him up. And maybe the door was already unlocked by then ...'

'Your lads saw nobody with him ...'

'They didn't actually *see* anybody. But then they were looking at your lad, parading about minus his pyjama bottoms. Doesn't mean there was nobody with him, who did a bolt when they saw our car ... anyway ...' He looked at me very hard and said,

'That night. Your missus wakened you out of your beauty sleep. And you knew exactly where to look for your lad. You went straight to the tower and straight up it, yelling for him. How do you account for that, Mr Clarke? How did you know where to look? Out of all the world, in the middle of the night?'

'I'd had him up there with me ...'

'That same day?'

'No, a few days before ...'

'Not good enough, Mr Clarke. You *knew*.'

I might have told him everything; but I knew how far I'd get, with a cynical little bugger like that.

'There's nowt more I can tell you.'

'Well, I can't make you tell me. And there's nothing I can hold you on. But there's something very nasty going on here, Mr Clarke, and I'm going to get to the bottom of it. Something kinky. I gather your lad's just getting over a nervous breakdown, can't remember anything. Keep in touch, Mr Clarke. Don't go running off to the Costa Brava for three months' holiday without letting me know, will you? Right, push off. I'm busy.'

I got up to go; I'd reached the door when he said, almost to himself,

'There's a trade in little lads these days. One time, it was only the little girls you had to worry over.'

I didn't know then how right he was.

The next morning, Billy and I went back to work on the tower. I mean, you have to, don't you? A Boeing 747 crashes and kills three hundred, but the other 747s go on flying; the day after a coach-crash which has killed ten grannies, the road is full of coachloads of grannies again. The world has to go on.

The only difference was, the cathedral green had more than its usual scatter of spectators watching us. There was nearly a hundred, that morning, and more as the day wore on. Ghouls! But it didn't make no difference to us. We had a job to do. Mind you, a high place where somebody has died is pretty bad; but I'd done it before, when one of my own lads came off a big chimney. He didn't check the top of the chimney properly before he started work on it; had a row with his missis before he left home that morning. Three bricks gave way – rotten mortar hidden by the soot – while he was standing on them. We helped get his body down off the factory roof, then got on with the job he hadn't finished.

Aye, it felt pretty black that morning, wi' the blood-splashes still on the nave roof because some bloody coward of a verger or mason hadn't had the guts to face them and scrub them away wi' a broom. But we ignored them, like we ignored the gargoyle. I got the rest of the rotten stone chipped out of the spire. Only we was extra careful; of the rope-sling, and of the wedges that were holding the ladders in place.

Mid-morning, we hears a shout from the parapet.

'Halloah! All right to come up?'

'Jesus,' says Billy.

'No,' I said, peering down. 'Only the Reverend Morris.'

'You'd think he'd have more sense, wi' his big gut. He'll break his bloody neck . . .'

'He's on his way,' I said. 'Coming up fast. I can't stop him. If he wants to be a bloody hero . . .'

'Give him a hand. I don't want the job of scraping *him* off the nave roof. What you think he wants?'

'Playing Sherlock Holmes, maybe. The scene of the crime.'

Morris made his own way, without any help, though I had to advise him about getting off the ladder on to the platform. He had to change from the outside of the ladder to the inside, and that got him in a right sweat; he hadn't reckoned on having to do that. He was shaking as he stood upright; both his hands gripped the top hand-rail as hard as I've ever seen it gripped. But he pretended to look round him, and sniff the morning breeze appreciatively and admire the wide view.

'All the kingdoms of the earth, and the glory thereof.'

'Aye, you don't get a bad view. What can we do for you?'

If he expected us to be impressed, he was wrong. To us it was no more than crossing a street; less dangerous, in fact.

'I've found out a bit more about this tower.'

'Oh, aye?' I tried very hard not to sound impressed.

'I won't tell you here though. There's things in books I want to show you. Suppose we say in the museum at one o'clock?'

'Fair enough.'

He looked down the tower at the ground. A thing I

don't particularly advise the nervous to do. It seemed to me his hands gripped the rail tighter still. Sooner I got him off the better. I didn't want him getting the shakes on us; he'd be a hell of a job to get down, if he did.

'I'm just going down to get some stone, Reverend,' I said. 'You can follow me down. I'll see your feet is set right.'

'The Lord shall lead your feet, into the paths of righteousness,' he said. But he was pale now, and a sheen of sweat had broken out on his forehead, though the wind up there was cool.

I led off, without further argument, and he came after me. I think I got him down to the parapet just in time. He was shaking like a great jelly by the time we got there. What the hell had he come up for, if he'd got no head for heights?

'I'd lay off heights in future,' I said. 'Some people feel at home there, some don't.'

'I'm at home anywhere, in the hands of God,' he said, a bit snappily.

I just thought, what do you have to pretend for? It's dangerous. You could get somebody else killed. What kind of God is it that makes you do things like that? But I didn't say anything; just, 'See you at one o'clock then.'

In the museum, he was his old self again: hand on my shoulder, booming voice. He had these huge calf-bound books out, thicker than a stone lintel and nearly as heavy. They were written in Latin that was double Dutch to me; great black handwriting with fancy letters.

He'd marked the places and he read out the Latin. Something about *aedificarunt* or something. He read them out because he enjoyed the sound of his own voice.

'Yeah,' I said, when he'd finished. 'Well?'

'Well what it means is that after the tower fell, they had three more shots at rebuilding it, in 1314, 1385 and 1414. And none of them got beyond roof-top height. Each one fell down. The foundations gave way. They weren't very good at foundations, I'm afraid, in the old days. Like at Winchester, where they built the cathedral on wooden piles driven down into a swamp. And when the wood began to rot . . .'

'I know the story,' I said. 'The Diver of Winchester.' That diver was one of my heroes. He spent a year down in the crypt of Winchester, underwater in his Victorian diving-suit, replacing the rotting piles with underwater concrete. The water in the crypt was black; he couldn't see more than a yard in front of him. And the water was full of decay from the rotting corpses in the church-yard. If he'd cut his bare hand while he was working, on an old nail sticking out or something, that would've been the end of him; a horrible death from blood-poisoning. But he saved the cathedral. I could never have done it; at least if you die up high, you die quick in a fall through clean air. I admire people who can do what I can't.

'To the greater glory of God,' said the Reverend Morris.

'Maybe he was just a pro,' said I.

He gave me a nasty look.

'Anyway,' he went on, 'the problem under the south-west tower was different. The old masons called it "the serpent in the sand".'

'Serpent in the sand?' I said. 'You mean, a bit like the Loch Ness monster?'

Another nasty look. 'Not quite. The whole cathedral is built on sand, you see. This is Cheshire. Half the buildings in Cheshire are built on sand. With rock-salt underneath that.'

'I know that. I've seen the sand quarries at Sandiway. And the salt-mine at Winsford. I was *born* here . . .'

'Sand and salt are safe enough, till you get underground water running through them, washing them away. That was the serpent in the sand – an underground spring welling up. When the old masons dug down after the tower fell, they found the remains of old water channels and caverns with smooth sides. They thought they were made by what they called the serpent in the sand. The springs came and went with the years, nobody could control them . . .'

'Salt subsidence,' I said, 'just salt subsidence.' But it made me feel uneasy just the same. What had happened once could happen again. I didn't much fancy working up that tower with water eating at the foundations, for all I knew, at this very minute. The sooner we were finished the job, the better.

He must've caught the look of worry on my face. He laid a great meaty paw on my arm again. 'Don't worry, Joe,' he said. 'That tower's stood for nearly five hundred years now. The architects have got all kinds of little devices that give warnings . . .'

I'd seen them. Little bits of glass fastened across cracks in the masonry, that break when the building shifts on its foundations. But it's a bit late to take to your heels, when you're up on the spire and a piece of glass cracks below ... you could be the filling in a masonry sandwich. Pressed beef, cooked bloody. But I wouldn't let him see I was worried, or he'd offer to pray for me at any moment, and I didn't want that. If I finished the job safe, it wouldn't be up to my common-sense any more. It'd be up to his prayers, and then I'd feel obligated and once you're obligated, anything can follow.

'Beats me how it's still standing,' I said.

'I can show you the man who made it stand,' he said. 'Come with me.' And he led me out into the cloister and then into the south aisle of the cathedral, with his hand on my shoulder. I was under spiritual arrest again.

The south aisle was dark; the pillars heavy and thick, Norman. The Norman windows were tiny. And full of stained glass. Mostly Victorian. I rather like Victorian glass, it's a good laugh wi' all those solemn, bearded faces and fat, floating saints in Roman togas. It tries so hard, and it's about as scary as a kid's comic book.

But there's some medieval glass as well. Muncaster has some of the best medieval glass left in this country, cos Oliver Cromwell didn't pass that way much. And you see some funny things in medieval glass. I don't think the medieval people were quite right in the head, half mad wi' the Black Death and starvation. And religion. Burning people at the stake for religion an' all that. Makes me glad that the Church is failing now, wi' dropping congregations and a dithering archbishop who doesn't know what he believes except he don't like

61

Thatcherism and neither do I. When the Church had power, it went on like a wild beast. Like them Muslim Fundamentalists still do.

'There he is,' says the Reverend Morris, swinging me round suddenly and pointing.

It was medieval glass all right. A crucifixion, small, but very nasty, all blood an' nails an' crown of thorns. Wi' people standing on each side. And on the right-hand side, a monk in black and white, wi' a tiny little cathedral in the crook of his arm, an' the cathedral had three spires, just like Muncaster.

'John of Salisbury,' announced the Reverend Morris. 'Last Abbot of Muncaster Abbey, before it was dissolved under Henry the Eighth. He knew trouble was coming; he was a man in a hurry for his God. He built the last tower, and it stands to this day.'

'Not a well-liked man, then,' I said.

'Why do you say that?'

'Someone's chucked a brick through his face.'

Where his face had once been, there was just a round patch of yellowy glass.

'Still, he's trampling down Satan under his feet,' said the Reverend Morris, pointing again. And indeed, under the figure of John of Salisbury was a crouched-up figure with a large face of incredible ugliness.

I went cold all over. The hairs rose on the back of my neck. Couldn't he see it?

That diabolical face of incredible ugliness was the same face as the face on the gargoyle of the south-west tower, give or take five hundred years of weathering and a lot of lichen.

And what's more, it wasn't a devil. In its too-small

hands it held, very tiny, a mason's punch-chisel in one, and a mason's hammer in the other. And what would Satan be doin' with a punch and hammer?

'That's him,' I said. 'That's him up the tower.' It just burst out of me, I couldn't stop it. There's times when you see a face, and you knows there's going to be trouble.

The Reverend Morris looked where my finger was pointing. He looked a long time before he said, 'Don't be silly, Joe. That stained glass would have been made in some workshop hundreds of miles away. The stained-glass men weren't living locally, like the masons. That window might even have been made in France or the Netherlands, to order, and shipped over years later. This is just a devil, a run of the mill devil.'

'A devil wi' a cold chisel and a mallet in his hands?' I said. 'I never heard of that afore. I'll tell you what you want to look for in those grand big books of yours, Reverend Morris. You want to look up the man that *really* built the tower for your John of Salisbury – the feller that sweated and schemed an' got his hands dirty. Not just the feller who gave the orders an' raised the money by trampling on the faces of the poor.'

He went on looking at that face, and so did I. In silence. He even reached up and touched the glass. Gave a little shiver. The shiver seemed to change his mind.

'I'll do what I can,' he said.

And there we left it.

We were starting to cement-in the new blocks on the steeple by the time our Kevin came out of hospital. They had no more reason to hold him; they could find nowt wrong wi' him. And he seemed quite normal as we drove him home. Looking forward to playing football wi' his mates an' getting back to school.

But Barbara and I were both uneasy, for very different reasons.

'I'm scared he'll start sleep-walking again,' said Barbara to me, as we settled down in front of the telly, leaving Kevin sitting reading in bed, upstairs.

'So am I. What d'you reckon we ought to do?'

'I think I want him to sleep in our bed . . .'

'Oh, go on, Barbara. He's a big lad now. An' he kicks an' snores. It's not like he was three years old still. We won't get a wink . . .'

'And I want you to sleep in his bed.'

That really made me fed up. She's very nice to snuggle up to, our Barbara. It's the one thing that can really make me feel safe. The buggers can't get to me, when I'm snuggled up to Barbara's back. Or so I delude myself.

But I knew she was right. Nothing had changed, really, since our Kevin first went walkabout in the middle of the night. And our Barbara's a very light sleeper. If he stirred, she'd know.

I lay awake a long time that night; restless for Barbara and finding Kevin's bed too soft. I was just finally drifting off when I heard Barbara yelling my name, frantic.

'Joe, help me, help me, I can't hold him.'

She was yelling from downstairs, by the front door. I went down those stairs so fast I tripped over me socks and nearly went headlong. The pair of them were fighting like fiends for the front door latch. As I watched, Barbara reached up and clamped her hand over it, and young Kevin opened his mouth, bared his teeth and bit her on the arm. I'll never forget the red blood trickling down her bare white arm. Only it looked black under the lights of our hall.

I grabbed Kevin, maybe harder than I should, cos o' that. He tried to bite *me*. His face was all teeth an' eyes screwed up shut with an expression of . . . I don't know what. I slapped him hard across the cheek, to bring him out of it; several times. But it didn't seem to have any effect. He just went on trying to bite me.

'That policeman-set he's got . . . them toy handcuffs. Get them, Barbara.' Toy handcuffs they might be, but made in Red China where they know how to make handcuffs. If those handcuffs went on you, there was no way you could get them off again, without somebody helping you.

She seemed a terrible long time finding them. Meanwhile we went on struggling. He was only eight, but he was slippery wi' sweat, an' his pyjamas nigh torn off him by that time, and he seemed to have the strength of ten, and cunning with it. By the time Barbara got back wi' the handcuffs, I was bleeding in three places, and he'd near gouged one o' my eyes out.

But I got them on him, an' the fight seemed to go out of him. He just sat on the bottom stair, panting wi' his eyes shut. Getting back strength to try again. It was Kevin's little body, that I'd seen so often in the bath; but it wasn't Kevin inside.

I got Barbara to fetch the nylon washing-line, an' I tied his ankles together with it, and then tied his ankles to his wrists behind him, but not too hard, not so as to

65

hurt him. When he felt the rope on his ankles, he started fighting again. Then when he knew it was no use, he stopped again. It was uncanny; it was like fighting a cunning little machine.

'I'll ring for the doctor,' said Barbara.

'No,' I said. 'I don't want him going to that hospital again.' It was too near that bloody cathedral, and sooner or later, some nurse would get careless and ... 'I want to get him right out of this,' I said. 'Let's go to your Margaret's.'

Margaret lives in mid-Wales. Even Kevin couldn't walk that far back to that damned cathedral.

'But Joe, they'll be asleep. It's the middle of the night ...'

'Then they'll have to bloody wake up. Go and get some clothes on, and bring me my big sheepskin, then go and start your car. You can drive, I'll hold him in the back.'

It was the most terrible journey of my life. Luckily her car's a Renault Five, with only two doors, so Kevin couldn't suddenly dive out without warning. But he could make a sudden dive for the back of Barbara's neck as we were driving along, tied up though he was. It was like driving along wi' a time bomb in the back; and a time bomb that could hurt itself too. His wrists were sticky wi' blood in the dark, where the metal had bitten into him, as he struggled.

It seemed a long time before she said, 'We're making progress. We're at Farndon.'

We knew Farndon well, from driving across to see their Margaret. It's a bit of a local beauty spot, on the banks of the River Dee; Farndon on one bank, and Holt over in Wales on the other. Two of the prettiest villages you could hope to see, wi' a fine medieval bridge spanning the river in between. I remember we crossed the bridge, under the lamplight. The river was running deep and black and smooth . . .

Then suddenly Kevin said, quite clear,

'Dad? Dad, where am I? My wrists hurt. And my legs.'

It was the real Kevin, back with us.

'Stop the car, Barbara.'

We pulled up in Holt. I took the cuffs off Kevin. He was frightened by the blood on his wrists, crying for his mum, and I didn't blame him, poor little bugger.

She spent a long time cuddling him. Then she said, 'He's all right now, Joe. Let's go home.'

I thought, then nodded to her, in the dimness of the courtesy light. It was still a hell of a long way to their Margaret's. And home's where everybody wants to be in the middle of the night, really. Specially when they're cold, hungry, exhausted and bleeding . . .

So she did a three-point turn, only it took seven points, and then we were heading back across the river to Farndon.

And as we reached the far bank, our Kevin went beserk again. Trying to get out of the car by crawling across my back for the door. We damned near crashed; missed a lamp-post by inches. Again I had to grab him, before he tore us to pieces.

I could think of only one thing.

'Get across that bloody river again.'

And as before, when we'd crossed, he relaxed and started to cry.

'Joe, for God's sake, what's up wi' him?' Barbara's eyes were wide as saucers, the whites showing all round. I could tell she was at the end of her tether.

'Nothing that water won't cure,' I said.

'What you mean?'

'We cross the river, he goes back to normal ... it's ... I read it in a book once. He'll stay normal, while we're across this river. We'd better go on to your Margaret's. I'd better drive ... you're clapped out.'

'Joe, what *kind* of book?'

I didn't want to answer her.

'Joe,' she insisted, her voice rising dangerously. 'What kind of book?'

I had to force myself to say it. It nearly made me sick, but I had to say it. 'A book on Black Magic,' I said, and felt a right idiot while I said it. 'Black Magic' used to be a brand of chocolates to us.

But she hadn't the strength left to argue. She just burst into tears and sat on the back seat hugging Kevin, and they cried themselves dry and then they fell asleep huddled together all the way to their Margaret's.

We knocked them up at five in the morning. I think they took one look at Kevin's wrists and one look at Barbara's face and nearly rang the police to report me as a child molester and general madman.

But I couldn't have cared less. Cos I'd suddenly been struck by a horrible thought.

The last time we saved our Kevin, another kid died. I couldn't wait to get on the blower to Muncaster police station. I asked for the duty inspector, and he was a very long time in coming. Which was as well, because

I was desperately trying to concoct a story for him that would make some kind of sense and get him to take some serious action, like checking on the lock of the south-west tower.

He came. He sounded uptight, but he heard me out. Then he said, very cagily, 'Could I have your name, sir?' Then he said, 'And your address?'

'I live near Muncaster, but I'm speaking from Aberystwyth.'

'Where in Aberystwyth?'

I told him.

'Can I have proof of that, Mr Clarke?'

What the hell did he want proof for? Was he nuts, or was I?

'I can put my brother-in-law on,' I said, irritably. 'He's Welsh enough for anybody. But what the hell for?'

'Just put your brother-in-law on, please.'

My brother-in-law spoke to him, convinced him I was where I said I was.

Then he asked my brother-in-law to put me back on.

'You'd better come back to Muncaster as soon as you can, Mr Clarke. We need to question you.'

My heart sank. 'Why, for God's sake.'

'We've just found another small boy dead. At the foot of the south-west tower.'

Allardyce looked up at me wearily when I finally stopped. The look on his old face was indescribable.

'Well, you asked me to tell you everything I knew,' I said. 'So I have.' What else was there to say?

'I believe every word of it,' he said. 'I was out in

Malaya during my national service. I was in the military police. There was a lot of funny stuff out in Malaya. Lads died, you filled in a report. You put down when they died, and where they died. But if you'd put down *how* they died – they'd have given you a medical discharge on the grounds of raving lunacy ... Malaya was the worst place in the world for it, you know. But you just filled in a form, and left that space blank, and left it to a higher authority. There's things the official mind just won't *take*, Mr Clarke.'

He got up, and made a futile attempt to tidy his desk. 'Meanwhile, we can keep a twenty-four watch on the door of that tower – have to, now – and that's all we can do. How long you going to be working on it, still?'

'Three more fine days will see it done – the stonework, that is. The weather-vane and weathercock – they're ready, but there's going to be a grand do. They'll be lowered into place by a helicopter from RAF Valley. *We* can do it perfectly well, but the RAF want their little moment of glory ... next Saturday. The whole town will be on the cathedral green ...'

'Their little moment of glory,' said Allardyce, dully.

I went home, though it didn't feel like home without Barbara and Kevin. It felt like a graveyard wi' curtains. I went to bed, and I slept badly. Dreams, dreams about that damned tower, but all jumbled up and making no sense. I wakened up towards evening, with a mouth like the bottom of a budgie's cage that hadn't been cleaned for a month; fried myself bacon and eggs, then couldn't eat it.

I remember it was a dull warm evening; nothing

moved in the greyness of the garden, not even a sparrow. I was locking up the house before going for a drink just to hear a human voice, when the phone rang.

It was the Reverend Morris. He sounded a bit uptight, like everybody else I had spoken to that day; but excited.

'I've got on to something in the records, Joe. I looked at where they started building – well, a bit before they started building really. And there he was – the chap you were talking about. The master mason. An Italian. Jacopo of Milan they called him.'

It figured. The face in the stained glass had been a foreign sort of face – big eyes and a beaky nose, and thin prominent bones – very dark.

'Can I come over now?' He sounded eager – hot on the chase.

Why not? It would save me going out and getting drunk. I could stay home and get drunk instead. 'Come over,' I said. Than I rang up Hughie Allardyce. He might as well hear it too. He was going on duty in a couple of hours, but he said he would look in, before he went to the station.

I got them out some lagers, though the Reverend Morris seemed scared to touch his; just pretending to be one of the boys, I suppose. On his knees was a mass of notes – sweat-crumpled sheets of paper with his big scrawly pencil-writing all over them.

'It's only a very rough translation from the Latin – I can do it better, given time. But it goes something like this . . .'

He paused, looked at us over his reading-glasses to make sure he had our full attention, then began.

71

'At that time ... the Abbot and the Brethren had despaired of the foundations of the south-west tower, for there was evidence that the serpent in the sand was present again, and doing the Devil's work for him.

'Then came one who called himself Jacopo Mancini of Milan, a master mason; though not one of us had ever heard of his name he had letters in his possession from three cardinals of the Church in Rome, recommending him as a worker of miracles in the art of building. And he told us that if we gave him his way and did all things according to his instructions, he could build a tower high and safe. And so the Abbot in his despair employed him and the craftsmen he brought with him, and gave them lodgings in the Abbey itself, for no lodgings could be found for them in the town, as they were hated as foreigners.

'And they worked, and the Abbot employed other masons from Chester and London, as none of the men of Muncaster would work with him. And there was fighting in the town, between the new men and the townsmen, because of the sins of pride and jealousy.

'But the tower arose without hindrance, though there was one strangeness in the building of it, that the masons left small ... the Latin says *Cella* ... cells? ... small rooms? ... small holes? ... at every stage of the work. And these were left empty when the masons from Chester and London went to rest at night, but in the morning they were found to be sealed up with heavy slabs, by the hand of the said Jacopo. And all the masons in the town asked what had been sealed in the ... *cella* ... and when the Abbot asked Jacopo he said writings of power to hold the tower up against the serpent in the sand, which were known only to him, nor would he let any other man look upon them, or his living would be gone. And the men of the town said they were charms of the Devil, but Jacopo told the Abbot they were taken from Holy Writ, in special places, such as the downfall of the walls of Jericho. But he would tell no more, not even though the Abbot pressed him hard.

'And when the tower was complete, the Abbot paid Jacopo what monies were due to him, and the said Jacopo departed and was never seen or heard of in this land from that time to the present; but the bodies of his two servants were found in the town, murdered so foully that none but one monk could recognize them, and he had been the one that fed them. Then stories were told in the town that they had been the very servants of the Devil himself, and that was Jacopo of Milan ... and there were affrays in the town against our Brethren and our house, and our Brother William of Sens was slain, and the men of the town foully cut off his head and played at football with it through the streets, and he was the one who had fed the servants of Jacopo of Milan. And the Abbot sent for the High Sheriff at Chester, who came and hanged some men of the town ... to wit Roger of Whitegate and his two sons, and John Mason and Thomas Carpeder ...'

The Reverend Morris sat back with a great gusty sigh of effort, nervously gathered his papers together, and waited for us to speak.

'Very nasty,' said Hughie Allardyce, lighting another cigarette with nicotine-stained fingers.

'There's *something* up there,' said the Reverend Morris. He was suddenly very excited; his small eyes were gleaming behind his gold-rimmed spectacles.

'I didn't think the Church held wi' that sort of talk,' I said abruptly. 'I didn't think your Church believed in Devils any more.'

'Perhaps the Archbishop of Canterbury doesn't,' he said, 'but *we* do. *We* see the Devil's work in the world. I have cast out Devils by prayer before this.'

'In church?'

'At meetings. We hold our own meetings. In people's houses ...'

I didn't like the sound of that at all. It sounded pretty unhealthy to me. All that singing and dancing and waving your arms in the air. Anything could happen to anybody at a meeting like that.

'I've found out a few things, too,' said Hughie Allardyce, quickly, as if he sensed a row was brewing.

I found that I was avid to hear what he had to say, too. It's infectious, that sort of attitude that the Reverend Morris had. That's why I don't like it.

'We've had the post-mortem reports on the two young lads who died. Not a mark on them, apart from the injuries sustained falling from the tower. They walked up to the top themselves – they weren't carried. We found the dust from the tower stairs on their feet. No sign of a struggle. And ...'

He scrabbled for another fag, with the one he had still burning in the ashtray.

'... I've been looking through the old newspaper reports, from the times the tower was repaired in the 1970s, the 1950s and the 1930s. In the 1950s, two little lads disappeared without trace. There was a national hue and cry. And in the 1930s, one of the masons murdered his own son; though it was reduced to manslaughter on appeal. He still got seven years for it.'

I shuddered, thinking how I'd had to treat Kevin. If things had gone wrong, I might have killed him . . . as if Hughie Allardyce had picked up my thought, he said,

'Your lad's still in Aberystwyth?'

'Where he'll stay wi' his Mam till this is all over.'

Hughie sighed with relief, and then settled again.

'What we goin' to do?' I said. 'The town's full of other people's bairns.'

'I'll have a day and night watch on that tower,' said Hughie, 'if I have to do it myself.'

'I shall talk to some friends of mine,' said the Reverend Morris. 'Real experts on this kind of thing. We'll get something together that can settle it . . .'

'And I'll get on wi' that stinkin' steeple,' I said. 'Sooner it's finished, the better.'

'Things always seemed to settle down again, once the work on the tower was finished,' said Hughie Allardyce.

But even then I knew we were kidding ourselves, with our sound common sense. I knew it wasn't going to be that simple.

Sunshine can be a mockery. I was hanging in bright sunshine now, in the rope-sling, fitting in the last few blocks of stone where the steeple had become rotten. By tonight, it'd be finished. And the weathercock and the weather-vane were gilded and ready, and gone in an RAF truck to the helicopter place at Valley. They were being put in place on Saturday afternoon, and tomorrow was Saturday. Then we could put a big new

lock on that tower door, and we'd be shot of our trouble
... or so I was trying to tell myself.

But I knew it wasn't true. I knew it wasn't true every
time my claw-chisel chewed into the stone of the steeple.
Those bloody masons down below seemed to have cut
every new block just that little bit too big; less than an
eighth of an inch. But that meant the block wouldn't
go in, unless I cut away a bit of the surrounding stonework. And every time I hit the stone, the chisel made
its ringing noise; and in the ringing noise, I could hear
the crying of children. But it was even more than that.
The whole tower and spire seemed to be ... thrumming
... every time the wind hit it. I could feel the forces
trapped inside the stone, wanting to break out. It was
like working on the outside of some great atomic missile
on its launching pad, sensing what was inside and what
it could do.

I kept on looking up at Billy; he looked quite normal,
having a little smoke, waiting to help me on to the next
bit. But he was smoking more than usual ... more than
the usual number of his fag-ends was sailing past my
head.

'They're late,' said Billy with satisfaction. 'Them helicopters cost ten million quid, and they're *late*.'

'Nice day for it,' I said, trying to keep calm, and not
keep on swallowing, as I looked at the crowd below.
The ring of spectators had grown to a hundred, two
hundred deep, so that the sharp corners of the cathedral
green were bending it out of shape. I could see choirboys
in their red and white, caught up in fascination on their
way back from sung daily evensong; a thin ring of

policemen in pale blue shirts, trying to keep the crowd back; the flashes from cameras, like a slow silent distant blue bombardment. Even the mayor was there, his robes of honour like a splash of blood.

'I wish to God they'd let us use the hoist,' said Billy. 'Wi'out all this fuss.'

'Amen to that,' I said. Using the hoist, we could've done the job in half an hour. A straight lift to the parapet (though the parapet hoist was playing up – gone very stiff, probably wi' rust. I should have greased the pulleys, but I hadn't got any grease handy.). Then up the spire by the spire hoist, with one of us steadying it from the ladders. The weather-vane was the awkward bit, with its six metal arms sticking out in all directions, up, down, north, south, east and west. It would have been a bugger to work through the top scaffolding, but we could have managed it, as we'd managed to get it down. (I shuddered, remembering its deadly journey down, when Billy had seen the first kid's body.)

Whereas working wi' this flashy helicopter was going to be a right bastard. For there was always wind round the steeple; nasty spiteful little gusts that tried to tug you off, this way and that, coming from any direction without warning, even on the quietest day. A steeple is like a sword raised against the wind; it makes turbulence. All buildings do, even smooth simple modern ones; but the cathedral was a lot worse, with its spider-work of pinnacles and transepts and buttresses, it could twist the wind into any shape.

And that without what was inside *this* particular steeple . . .

'Look at them,' said Billy. 'Look at all them ghouls ...'

The cathedral green was full now; you couldn't see the grass any more; it was covered with humans, crawling wi' them, like a chucked-out chicken leg crawls wi' flies.

'I hope they get what they've come for,' said Billy bitterly, and I found my stomach tightening. Then he cocked an ear and said, 'Here it comes.'

There was the slight faint blatting of a helicopter, and we heard a satisfied murmur rise from the crowd, like a sigh, so far below it was.

The blatting grew louder, echoing around Cathedral Close's tall buildings, so there seemed half a dozen helicopters not one.

'Check my sling, Joe,' said Billy nervously. I checked his safety-sling, the other end fastened to the scaffolding, and then he checked mine.

The helicopter was coming in about a hundred feet above us, the gilded weather-vane dangling beneath it like a great obscene fish-hook, and the RAF bloke looking out of the big hatch in the side, judging the distance, telling the pilot what to do through his throat microphone. I took a look at the pilot; he looked a steady intent chap; I liked the careful way he watched what he was doing.

Then the chopper was right overhead, and Billy's mouth was opening and shutting and I couldn't hear a word he was saying, for the noise of the chopper's engine and blades. Every blat of it hit your ears like a fist, making you want to cower. I began to wish we'd used ear-plugs, but it was too late now. And the pressure from the rotor blades coming downwards, pushing you flat so you had to struggle to keep your balance. Never again, I told myself; then the weather-vane was on its way down to us, swinging like a pendulum, not far or fast, but I remembered the weight of it.

Billy and I were just reaching up to steady it, and guide it into the socket on top of the steeple we'd got ready for it . . .

When it happened.

The weather-vane swung out away from us, dipped a few feet, swung back far too low, and caught under the scaffolding with a terrible clang. The scaffolding was hooked like a fish. And in a flash, the rising air had pushed the helicopter upwards again.

The whole scaffold heaved up under us like the deck of a ship when a wave hits it. There was a terrible grating as it tried to break free of the steeple. We were thrown on our faces; without the safety-slings, we'd have gone clean over the edge of the planking.

But it was worse for the helicopter. I think there should have been a safety cut-out on their lowering-hook. All I could tell people afterwards was that if there was it didn't seem to work in time. The whole helicopter tilted; there was a screech of metal on metal as one of the rotor blades must've hit our scaffolding. Then it was falling away, leaving the weather-vane stuck with us. Still flying, but with the end snapped off one of its rotors. Flying as wild as a dragon-fly, flitting and twisting and turning over the upraised faces of the crowd, caught in the narrow, tall space of the cathedral green.

All we could do was lie there and watch. All I can say is that, going on the way he fought to save it crashing on the crowd, that pilot must've been a hell of a good pilot and a very brave man.

The crowd never moved; just a sea of faces staring up, paralysed at all that metal and aviation fuel hanging above them.

It seemed to go on for ever, and then the chopper reached the edge of the crowd, tried to lift above the Bishop's Palace and crashed into the roof, sending up a fountain of red roofing tiles.

Thank God it didn't catch fire.

Now the crowd began to move. Swirls and twists of people fighting to escape; crashing into each other like a pan of black peas come to the boil.

When the green was finally empty, there were still bodies lying all over the turf.

And at that moment, the scaffolding lurched under us again, with a terrible grating noise.

'Christ,' said Billy. 'It's going.'

'What happened?' asked Hughie Allardyce. 'Take your time.' His voice was strangely gentle, almost like a woman's. It helped me to start talking again.

'We tried to edge our way towards the ladders. We had to move one at a time, balance each other. If we'd both moved together, it would have gone straight away. He let me move first. He trusted me. He was my mate. We'd been together five years ...'

'I'm sure you did your best for him,' said Hughie.

'The worst of it was that nobody had noticed *us*. All them sirens – ambulances, police cars – we might as well have been on a different planet.'

'The fire brigade had nothing that would have reached you,' said Hughie.

'Anyway ... I didn't notice at first that I was moving further each time than he was. I was shit-scared, so I don't know how scared he must have been. I had to talk him into moving at all, every time. I think his nerve was gone. I could bear to move a foot at a time, he'd do about six inches. After that, he was close to blackin' out. I just tried to keep on talking to him.

'Anyway, I reached the ladder, and crawled aboard inch by inch. I was frightened that once my weight went off the scaffold, the whole shooting match would go down. But it didn't. The ladders were firm enough *then* ...

'By the time he got within reachin' distance, all the police and ambulances was gone – it was very quiet and the sun came out. As if nothing had happened ... it was obscene.

'Then I noticed his safety-sling was caught round the scaffold. He'd have to cut it. I'd cut away mine already, so's I could reach the ladders. I managed to pass him my knife, at the third attempt. And then when he began to cut his sling, his hands were so weak, he dropped the knife. I watched it dwindle away down to the parapet, and bounce off on to the green.

'After that, there was nothing to do but try and get him on to the ladder, so I could untie the knots for him myself. I got him on ... then I found I couldn't untie the knots. They'd tightened, and my own hands were too weak and shaking so much. He just kept on saying, "Have you managed it, Joe? Have you managed it?" Still trusting me. And I could do nothing for him,

81

nothing at all. I think he guessed in the end. He said, "It's no good, Joe, is it?" Then he began to get the shakes . . . and there was only one end to that – for both of us, if I didn't move myself. So I said, 'I'll go down and get help, Billy. We'll get the fire brigade up to you in a jiffy." And he said,

'"All right, Joe, see you in a bit." And I climbed down very slowly to the parapet and he was still OK up there. So I shouted, "See you in a bit," and started down the spiral staircase.

'I hadn't gone twenty steps down when I heard the whole caboodle break loose up top, and fall. He was there on the green, covered in scaffolding, when I reached the bottom. There wasn't a mark on him; but he was dead.'

'I'm sorry,' said Hughie Allardyce. 'You did all you could.'

'I left him alone to die.'

'Would he feel any better now if you'd died with him?'

'I could've had one more go at them knots . . .'

'No you couldn't. And you know it.'

'If you say so,' I said, hating him for a minute.

There was a long silence, and then I made a great effort and said, 'What happened – to the rest of them?'

'Nobody dead. Bloody miracle, the way that pilot kept a grip on his chopper. He's going to be OK – two broken legs. The helicopter winchman's in intensive care, but they've got some hopes for him. Three more in intensive care, from the crowd – kids. The rest are crush-injuries – broken ribs and legs. If that chopper had crashed on the crowd and caught fire, we could've had a hundred dead ...'

There was another long silence. Then I said,

'It wasn't an accident. That tower would like to kill the whole town, and it damned near did.'

'Don't talk daft, Joe. Don't talk like that. You're upset.' That was the Reverend Morris talking; he'd sat quiet till now; he was very thoughtful, for him.

'What're people saying in the town?' I asked.

'An accident, a ghastly accident. There's a lot of bad feeling towards the RAF. And the cathedral. We're getting the blame. They want occasions like that abolished. People have rung up their MPs ...'

'And about the two little lads?'

'They're saying the second kid was a copy-cat of the first. Once they knew there was no evidence of foul play ...' Hughie too looked very thoughtful. 'People believe what they want to believe. They'd never believe what we think happened.'

'So it's up to us,' I said.

'Steady on,' said Hughie. 'What do you mean, it's up to us?'

'I've spoken to my people,' said the Reverend Morris. 'They think we can do something; but not before next weekend. These things take time ...'

'Meanwhile,' I said, 'how many more kids are goin' to die?'

'I've got one of my lads watching that tower day and night. Two in a panda at night.'

'And suppose there's a car-crash in Cathedral Close? Or a mugging or some girl screaming? Will your fellers still just sit there, watching the tower door?'

Hughie shifted uneasily in his chair.

'I'm going to settle that bloody tower's hash tonight,' I said. 'I know where to look. You'll have to arrest me if you want to stop me, Hughie. It's killed my mate, an' it nearly killed my lad, an' it's getting hungrier all the time.'

'I'm coming along,' said Hughie. 'I don't want another dead steeplejack on my conscience. And at least I can stop my lads arresting you ...'

'I'm coming too,' said the Reverend Morris. We all suddenly stood up together, there in my dim little kitchen. It was unreal, the way we all stood up together. And yet, in that moment, we became three mates.

'Do you mind if I say a prayer first?' asked the Reverend Morris.

I nearly said I didn't want any of that stuff. But you don't spit on a mate, or on what a mate believes in. So I said, 'OK. But make it quick. We haven't got all night.'

Even though we had got all night.

It was funny, while he was praying. I couldn't close my eyes; I kept staring at the daft pattern on the kitchen floor tiles. And yet his praying was so like he was talking to somebody in the room ... I almost believed there was a fourth bloke with us in the room. And if He was there, I wasn't sorry to have a bit of help. I'd have accepted help from Old Nick himself against that tower. And he spoke to this guy he was talking to so personal, like he was a friend; and he cared about *me*, and Billy and Kevin and Barbara. I could've wept. Only you can't afford to weep when you've got a job to do; weep after, if you like.

Then the Reverend Morris went and got his Bible from his car, and I went to get a seven-pound sledge-hammer from the shed.

'The hammer of the Lord, and of Gideon,' said the Reverend Morris. He gave a ghost of a smile, to show me it was some kind of shot at a joke. And Hughie said roughly,

'Let's get started then. We'll take my car. It's got a radio, so I can radio for a bloody ambulance ...' And that was his kind of joke.

Funny. I didn't reckon much to old Hughie, usually. Nor the Reverend Morris. But we were three that night, going to do something, and that was all that mattered.

There was a police cordon across the entrance to the cathedral green, where the tail of the crashed helicopter still stuck out of the roof of the Bishop's Palace. Plastic ribbons twisting in the wind, and a panda, and two bored coppers who were nosier than I liked. We'd never have got through, but for Hughie.

But no one watching the tower door, closer to. I'd been right, they weren't being careful enough.

While they were moving the barriers, I looked across to the west front of the cathedral. The street-lamps cast their yellow light upwards on to it, fading slowly as it climbed, so that the twin steeples were in darkness, just tall black points against the sky. It seemed to me then that the two towers were quite different. The harmless north-west tower was clear-cut in the yellow light, just an empty needle of stone. But the other ... it seemed to my eye darker, as if it half-repelled the light ... crumblier, almost ... furry. I rubbed my eyes, because

I don't like that kind of delusion. But it didn't do any good.

We drove across and parked.

'I've still got a key,' said Hughie, fumbling in his overcoat pocket. He put the key into the lock, and tried to turn it. 'Bastard won't turn. Lock's jammed.'

'Never did that afore,' I said. And my heart leapt. It was like when you were squaring up for a fight, in the old days, with a bloke who was bigger and nastier than yourself, and you reckoned you didn't have much chance. Until you feinted with your left at him, and he jumped back a bit too quick, in a way that told you he was scared too, and that you had a chance of licking him.

The tower was a bit scared of us. It didn't rate our company that night. Though whether it was scared of the Reverend Morris and his invisible Friend and his Bible, or me and my hammer ... anyway, Hughie went on fiddling with the key, and I had a go, and then the Reverend Morris. And when we saw it was hopeless I said, 'Stand back,' and then before anybody could move, I hit the lock with the hammer, with all my strength and all my hate.

Steel and stone screeched like a living thing; and I hit it twice more, for good measure, and it banged back and there was broken stone lying all over the pavement.

'Bloody hell,' said Hughie. 'Who's going to explain *that* to the Super in the morning?'

He went first; we all had big flashlights. The wall and steps of the spiral stair were wet and clammy, as if something was sweating. And our torches and our arms and legs threw shadows, as if we struggled up through a mass of writing dark flat worms. The air was close and stale and warm and damp. It seemed to push down on us, so that the stairs seemed never-ending, as if we were in the belly of a stone beast, and had very little hope of ever seeing the light of day again. The Reverend Morris began to sing some sort of little hymn at that point, the same words over and over again. I'd have called it a silly pointlessness at any other time. But it was a good sound to climb steep twisting stairs to, in the middle of the night, so I joined in, and I think Hughie did to. It helped, like a dirty song does on an army route march.

It was then that I noticed something I'd never noticed before. The spiral stair had little landings on it, every complete twist through three hundred and sixty degrees. And on the landing, under the lancet window that lit the stairs by day, was a stone ledge jutting out of the wall. And I began thinking of that word *cella* that had been in the Latin writings the Reverend Morris had translated. Those *cellas* must've been left where the masons could reach them easy; why not on the spiral stair?

'Hang on,' I said, and inspected the next ledge thoroughly.

The top was a stone slab; and on the slab was a mason's mark; several mason's marks, and none of them known to me; they had a foreign look.

'Something?' asked Hughie. His voice seemed to echo away up the stone spiral. Something, something, something, something, coming back off every turn of the wall.

'Maybe,' I said, and got as good a swing on the

hammer as I could, in that confined space, and hit the jutting-out corner of the ledge.

Sparks flew; the slab broke free from the surrounding stonework and moved out a couple of inches, leaving a wedge of darkness below. And out of that wedge of dark came a stink, the like of which I'd never smelt in my life.

'Dead rat?' gasped Morris, gagging on his own breath.

'Dead rat nothing,' I said, reversing the sledge-hammer and using the handle as a lever to widen the crack of darkness.

Then we shone a torch down; down a deep narrow slot about ten inches wide.

Something shone in the light of the torch. Something round and white like an oversized billiard-ball, only with strands coming out of dark holes, strands of shining grey that seemed to grow into the stonework. Like a spider's web, but with much thicker strands. More like the roots of some plant. But the round billiard-ball thing . . .

'A . . . skull,' said Hughie Allardyce. 'A little . . . child's . . . skull.' And hardened policeman that he was, he turned away and threw up, down the spiral stair. You could hear the spew splashing away, down below.

But I looked further. There was more than a skull; there was a whole tiny skeleton wedged down into the narrow slot, still sitting with its knees forced up near its head, and its arms folded in between. And down below, the grey shining strands grew thicker and thicker through the bones, tying the tiny form to the stone.

'The miracles of Jacopo of Milan,' said Morris in a very small voice.

'Aye,' I said. 'The Abbot got what he wanted. At a price. No wonder they smashed his face out of that stained-glass window.'

'He could never have known ...'

'He never even bothered to find out. He got his tower. That was enough for him.'

'I can't believe ...'

'Oh, c'mon,' I said. 'Any cathedral was built on the deaths of children. Where d'you think the money came from? How else could they afford to build, in a country where half the people nigh starved to death every winter? The money came from the workers, and the workers' children starved. Every stone must be a death, nearly. To the glory of God. This Jacopo just had a new recipe, that was all.'

But he wasn't listening any more. His face, in the torchlight, was an agony of pity. 'This child ... can't have been more than eight or nine.'

'Maybe older. You stay small, when you're starving ...'

'This ... stuff ... growing on it. It's like a plant. Is it dry rot?'

'No, it's not dry rot. I've seen dry rot at its worst. It's never like this. I reckon it's taking the goodness out of the child, feeding it into ... the stone. All these years ...'

His hand reached down into that dreadful space. I think he had some thought of rescuing the tiny frail bones. Something ... the very look of the strands warned me.

'Don't touch it!'

But it was too late. He was trying to pull the thick strand from the tiny knees.

The next second, he screamed.

I grabbed his shoulders and pulled him back. His shoulders were as rigid as a board. The strand tore, and came away with his hand. The torn piece writhed, as if it was trying to dig into his flesh. There was blood on his hand, then red raw flesh, then a glint of white bone, as he held it up before his face. Then the piece of broken strand writhed once more, then curled up rigid and fell back into the slot where the child lay.

'God,' said Hughie, 'half the flesh of his hand is gone.'

'Get him out, quick! Get an ambulance! He could lose that hand. Go on, get moving,' I shouted.

'What about you?'

'I'll be all right,' I shouted. 'I know now. I *know*!'

He gave me a white-faced look, and led the stumbling Reverend Morris back down the spiral stair.

I listened to their retreating footsteps, until there was silence. Then I went on up that stair, by the light of my solitary torch, with my sledge-hammer in my other hand.

'All right, mate,' I said to the walls. 'Don't you worry. I'm coming, I'm coming. I'm coming as quick as I can, you bastard.'

Just for a second, I could have sworn I felt the whole tower sway around me. Towers do sway, of course, like chimneys do – in a high wind; when the bells are rung. But there was no sound of wind tonight; and no bells were being rung.

He knew I was coming for him.

I reached the parapet door. It seemed to be locked or jammed. I smashed it open with one blow of the hammer, and stepped out into the clean smell of the night. It wasn't all the smell of plants and growing things; there was soot in it, and chemicals. But after that stair, it smelt as good as the air in the Outer Hebrides.

Far off, I could see the police panda at the entrance to the cathedral green, and two figures standing by it. Hughie and the Reverend Morris were safe, then. Further off, I could hear a siren. Maybe the ambulance was on its way. But it was all a long way off, and no longer anything to do with me really.

Just me and the gargoyle; the gargoyle of Jacopo of Milan, worker of miracles in the art of building; with letters of praise from three cardinals of Mother Church.

'Aye well,' I said. 'You knew your trade, Jacopo. And I know mine.'

And I raised the sledge-hammer as if it was an executioner's axe, and brought it down on the rotten stone behind the gargoyle.

And as the stone fell in a yellow, rolling crumble at my feet, I smelt the smell again, the smell they'd all talked about, over all the years.

I got all the rotten surface blocks off first. I wasn't in any hurry, and I didn't want to go blundering into anything clumsy-like; especially not the stuff that had done for the Reverend Morris.

Then I began to smash in deeper.

The gargoyle-head broke loose, as its support fell away, and rolled under my feet. It got in my way, almost as if it was trying to trip me up and send me reeling over the parapet.

'Careful, Clarke,' I said to myself. 'Careful, Clarke!'

It was not that I was afraid; but I had a job to do, and I meant to finish it in a workmanlike way, like I'd always done.

But under my feet, I felt the tower sway again. As if there was a wind, and yet there was no wind.

I knew I'd broken through, when the smell really hit me. Even in the open air, I was nearly as sick as poor Hughie. When I got the torch, from where I'd left it shining on the parapet to light my way, I saw that a big crack had developed in the stonework of the corner of the lower steeple, where the gargoyle had been. Again I reversed the hammer, and inserted it in the crack, and levered.

A whole side fell away.

And there he squatted, as a man might squat on a primitive privy. Stuffed inside the stone, as he had stuffed his victims. Alive, buried alive, I'd have guessed. For he wasn't a skeleton, as his victims had become skeletons. He was much worse than any skeleton. He was alive as a turnip in the ground is alive. Half skeleton, and half obscene bulging turnip, with a great thick root running down between his skeleton legs into the stone. A root thicker than a man's ...

I nearly threw up then.

Did he look at me? Can a turnip look at you?

But he was aware of me, I swear. That's why I spoke to him; so he would know for sure.

'No, I'm not touchin' you,' I said to him. 'I'm not such a fool as that. No, I'll leave the sun to touch you, and the rain, and the clean air. I'm not a fool like the Reverend Morris. An' I'm not a fool like them that buried you alive an' left you in the stone to die. That was the worst day's work they ever did, poor sods, God rest them. No, we'll see what the sun will do to you. It'll be up in a few hours. You can wait till then. You can think about it. Sun's hot. It'll dry you up by inches, an' no one'll even hear you scream.'

I think he understood. For just then the tower gave a great shudder; and the steeplejack in me warned me it was going. Maybe, down there, the serpent in the sand was loose again. Maybe what had held the tower up for centuries was giving way.

'Starting to despair, are you?' I spat in at him. 'I'm *glad.*'

And then, horribly, I realized that he wanted me for his last victim. If I started down the spiral stair now, the tower would fall when I was half-way down, and I'd be crushed to pulp, and his roots would come and eat my pulp, and God knew where my soul would be.

I knew I wouldn't do it. I'd rather jump from the parapet and die in clean air. I'd jump as far out as I could, so the fallen stone would not enclose my bones, and he wouldn't get me. That was the way to do it.

The tower swayed again; it was time to go.

I was gathering myself for the jump; thinking a last sad quick thought about our Barbara and Kevin, when I saw it.

The rope of the parapet hoist, hanging loose, the sling on the end of it empty. The parapet hoist that was stiff and slow-working, with the rusty pulley. Maybe it was just stiff enough to slow my fall . . .

I didn't give myself time to think, time to panic. I leapt outwards and grabbed the empty sling with both hands. I began to drop quickly. And then when I was half-way to the ground, the pulley above my head began to screech like a harpy and I felt my fall slowed. The sling nearly pulled my arms out of their sockets, but I clung on somehow.

And then the pulley seized up solid, when I was about twenty feet from the ground. But I just trusted to luck and let go and dropped. Well, I think my arms gave way really, I had no choice. But I remembered to bend my legs and roll as I hit the ground.

A man can survive a drop of twenty feet; landing in a parachute is like dropping from seventeen feet, and I've done that.

I just felt as if both my legs were broken.

But I got up and *ran*. Ran before the tower fell on me. Because all the way down, I'd seen the cracks in its walls growing upwards like black lightning, in the yellow light of the street-lamps.

And I ran like bloody hell; because I somehow knew that whichever way I ran, the tower would fall after me. Just like a great factory chimney, laid to within an inch of its target.

As I ran, I felt the tremor in the earth; I heard the rumble starting in my ears. How high was the spire? How far was it across the cathedral green to the entrance where the panda car stood? All the way across the green, hobbling like a madman, I kept doing those sums in my head.

Nearly there. If I could turn the corner into Cathedral Street, there was hope for me. My lungs were going like old bellows, but above them I could hear the rumble of the fall. She'd be coming down slow and graceful, reaching for me, reaching for me. Like a leaping tiger. I could smell her smell now, the disturbed dust of centuries, swept past me by the wind of her falling.

I didn't make it. I ran into the shop doorway of Harrison's the Stationers by mistake, in my sweaty-eyed panic and blindness. I turned in that doorway, and watched her come. Graceful as a woman lying down, blowing her black cloud of smoke before her.

And then, oh glory, she was falling short of me. She was running out of spire. I could see the very top about to hit the earth, twenty yards in front of me. Even allowing for rebounding stones, I had a chance . . .

And then out of the black smoke of falling it came. My death. The gargoyle-head itself, bounding and roll-ing and leaping like an animal, with all the force of gravity in the world behind it. Like a black misshapen cricket ball, bowled by the biggest fast bowler the world had ever seen.

'Oh God,' I said. So near and yet so far. Barbara. Kevin.

The gargoyle-head leapt at my face.

And I had the wit to duck.

And it leapt over my bent body, and straight through the plate-glass door, and I heard it rolling and rattling to rest among the racks of Harrison's stationery.

And then there was shouting and policemen running, and lights going on all over Cathedral Close.

Hughie Allardyce looked really stupid with a bunch of

flowers in his hand, sitting by my hospital bed. But I was pleased to see his old face.

'Rather have had chocolates,' I said, to keep my end up.

'That's why I brought flowers,' he said, to keep his end up. 'Well, you certainly settled the tower. They're still shovelling it up. Eight days, and that's wi' bulldozers. Twenty thousand tons, they reckon the stone weighed. What the hell did you do? Blow it up wi' jelly?'

'I showed our friend the light of day. An' he didn't fancy it. So he sort of gave up. Was there any ... trace?'

'The contractors haven't reported finding owt unusual. I expect everything was crushed by the falling stone. Crushed to bits. They haven't even found those bones we saw ...'

He shuddered delicately. 'I can't believe I ever saw them. It just seems like a bad dream now ...'

'What're they doing with the stone?'

'Crushing it and using it as hardcore for a hypermarket car-park out Sandeston way. He'll be buried under a foot o' Tarmac.'

I lay back and smiled. I liked that idea very much.

'They're not blaming you,' he said. 'The architect reckons that the foundations gave way. Underground springs.'

'Salt subsidence, I expect. Anyway, nothing for you to put into a report.'

'Nothing for me to put in a report,' he echoed.

'Between you and me,' he said, 'half the stuff that happens in the world goes into reports, and half doesn't.

And it's the important part that doesn't.'

'How's the Reverend?'

'They've managed to save his hand. He'll need a lot of skin-grafts though. And his cricket days are over. So are his vicaring days, apparently. He's thinking of training to become a social worker.'

'That'd be a pity,' I said thoughtfully. 'When that gargoyle was heading straight at me, someone told me to duck, in time. Except there was nobody there ... I thought it might have been some Friend of his ...'

'Never know, do you?' And with that, he got up and went. Hasn't got much time for religion, Hughie Allardyce.

As for me, I've still got time for steeplejacking.

But no more cathedrals; I'll stick to chimneys in future.

Brangwyn Gardens

Students lived off the fat of the land in 1955. The full grant was two hundred and fifty a year, and you could live in London very nicely on five pounds a week, including a good night out on a Saturday night.

And yet Harry Shaftoe was a bit mean, like many of the male students. Every term he changed his digs to avoid paying the landlady a retainer over the vacation. Every start of a new term, he turned up at the Lodgings Office to ask for a new list of addresses. The Lodgings Officer was sick to death of him; which was why she gave him the address in Brangwyn Gardens.

Nobody stayed long in Brangwyn Gardens; as she gave Harry the address, she also gave him a look that said so. Harry thought he knew what to expect: squalling kids, a dotty landlady, even half-full piss-pots standing all day in the hall. He didn't care; he didn't see why he should pay landladies his own good money for doing nothing, for keeping his room idle. He was used to roughing it; his back was broad.

But Brangwyn Gardens wasn't at all what he expected. Brangwyn Gardens had been rather grand; a tall, early Victorian terrace near the open greenery of Parliament Hill Fields. He could walk in to the Slade from there.

Except that the bombers had come to Brangwyn Gardens at the height of the Blitz, cutting the terrace into segments as easily as a grocer cuts cheese. And number eleven stood quite alone, like an elegant severed head. A severed head, thought Harry a bit wildly, held up on crutches. For two houses had gone from its left, and three from its right, leaving a series of low bricky mounds where blitzweed grew to near shoulder height, and out of those scrawny grey-green bushes, with their drifting loads of old man's beard, reared the vast baulks of timber that held number eleven upright. The baulks had been there so long that they in their turn had grown old; riven with damp cracks, and stained with the streams of rust that grew out of the nuts and bolts that held them together, which looked like old bloodstains.

Number eleven itself looked very spruce: the Doric pillars that framed the door were newly painted, and so were the many sash windows; but it just looked like cosmetics on a carefully made-up severed head.

That was the front; the sides of the house hadn't been touched since 1940. Strips of bleached wallpaper, high up on the long-gone fourth floors of numbers nine and thirteen still stirred in the breeze. Up there, there was still a bathroom mirror screwed to the wall, glinting in the afternoon sun; and the cistern of a long-gone toilet, and a white hand-basin, clinging to the ancient scarred brick like strange white limpets.

Harry screwed up his face in distaste. As a little kid, in the Blitz, he'd enjoyed such strangenesses. But all that was old hat now; he hadn't thought of such things for years. Now his life was the new sculpture of Henry Moore and his own tutor at the Slade, Reg Butler; foreign movies and thoughts of girls.

Sadly, it wasn't a girl who opened the door of number eleven to his ring. Just a landlady, and odder than most. A landlady in a headscarf, though it was tied behind her head in the upper class way, not in front like the workers did it. Thick pebbly glasses, behind which her muddy eyes swam away furtively like unattractive goldfish startled by the light. Thick lumpish grey cardigan, washed till it had pilled across the front and under the armpits. Below, lumpy navy slacks, shiny with age, and black lace-up shoes. Harry, from long and bitter experience, crossed her off the list of the human race and said, 'I've come about the room.'

'Oh yes, the room,' said the woman. 'I'm afraid it's on the top floor. I hope you don't mind an attic?' But she didn't say it *to* him. She was already swimming away into the gloom of her hall. Harry picked up his battered suitcase and holdall and went in pursuit. Laden as he was, he had a hard time catching up with her. She must not be quite so decrepit as she looked. Steep flights of stairs, dark and highly polished, succeeded each other. It felt like climbing up inside the Great Pyramid of Cheops. Strange and exotic items floated past him as he panted upwards. A grandfather clock, ticking loudly and slowly. Three cases of stuffed fish, screwed to the wall one above the other. A great white polar bear rearing up to threaten him. The stair-carpet was soft and thick under his feet, so that he climbed in silence, apart from the sound of his own panting. He had a sense of leaving the world behind, climbing into silence and darkness.

Then suddenly there was a blaze of light above and ahead, and the landlady's dumpy form silhouetted in a doorway.

'This is it.' She stood aside to let him pass. He dumped his bags on to a narrow bed, and straightened up, hands digging into his aching back.

The view was wonderful. Through huge brick chimneys, a distant blue view of the dome of St Paul's. He'd always wanted a view of St Paul's, but in all his wanderings from lodging to lodging, he'd never had one. You only really felt you were in London when you had a view of St Paul's ...

For the rest, the room was long and narrow, with sloping ceilings and two dormer windows. He'd always wanted a room with dormers, a real artist's garret ... and besides the narrow bed, there were two nice old lath-back rocking chairs and clippie rugs on polished floor-boards.

What a room to bring a girl to! He'd never had a girl, beyond talking to them, or doing the jive with them at the Friday night Slade hop. Alone with girls, he grew tongue-tied. But up here, the alone-ness far above the world and the dormer windows with their view of St Paul's might do his talking for him ...

'How much is it?' he asked, already knowing he'd take it.

'Thirty shillings a week. Week in advance. Week's notice either side.' The woman was staring at his scuffed old bags, lying on the bed, as if she was learning all she needed to know of her new lodger from them. Nervously she put up her hand and tucked a stray strand of dark hair back inside her headscarf. As she did so, he noticed her ear. It was absurdly fine and shapely, on such a mess of a creature. But then he'd noticed such things before. His Auntie Daisy, his mother's older sister, had beautiful shapely legs. No varicose veins or anything, though she was over sixty. Those beautiful legs haunted him at family Christmas parties; they went so ill with that grey hair and that high-pitched cackling laugh (over women's dirty jokes muttered in corners after the port wine had gone round twice). He had an absurd desire to rescue those beautiful legs and return them to their rightful owner, who would be satisfyingly grateful . . .

He reached inside his coat to get out his wallet.

'Don't pay me now,' said the woman hurriedly, though she hadn't looked at him. 'Pay me when you come downstairs again. I'll fill out your rent-book.' Then she was gone.

The room only began to seem odd as he unpacked and wandered round exploring it, shirts or jumpers or pyjamas in his hands.

Behind the sun-faded floral curtains lurked black-out curtains, with cobwebs and the transparent bodies of flies and even spiders still in their rigid folds. There was a wartime identity card on the mantelpiece of the cast-iron fireplace, made out in the name of Colin Borden, born 18/1/23. Behind the door hung a soldier's greatcoat with a corporal's stripes. And on top of the coat hung a soldier's gas mask case with steel helmet still attached, the way they'd carried them in the War. The greatcoat and gas mask and helmet annoyed him especially; they made it hard to get the door more than half open. He wondered if he dared move them. Landladies could be funny if you moved their things. He remembered hideous purple vases and huge plaster Alsatian dogs that he'd removed and hidden in drawers in previous digs, only to find them resurrected when he returned from college and put back in place; and how the landlady's manner had turned suddenly freezing. He'd once been thrown out in the middle of a term after a protracted battle over three flying ducks; the woman had literally screamed at him; been foaming at the mouth . . . and her husband had been very nasty too and thrown his bags down the stairs . . .

He'd better go and ask. And pay his rent at the same time. He descended the endless dark stairs, paid his respects to the bear whom he christened 'Horace'. Though that didn't change the expression of diabolical malevolence on its face as it dismembered a wretched penguin between its claws under the dim light of the forty-watt bulb on the landing. He had a funny idea that polar bears only lived at the North Pole, and penguins only at the South, which would make Horace or the unfortunate penguin very well-travelled . . . but somehow in the face of the bear's expression, the joke wilted and died. He had to knock on several doors when he reached the ground floor, before he got a response through one. He was beginning to realize what a huge house this was. Was he the only lodger? It was so silent, and by his watch it was now well past five; time for people to be home from college or work, doors to be open, insults and moans to be exchanged, or at least good evenings said. But the hall remained dark, shining, polished and empty.

Anyway, she called a muffled 'Come in' and he gave her two pound notes without looking at her. It was *kinder* not to look at her; those terrible pebble-like glasses; that prim, pale mouth without a trace of lipstick, like a dead thing; that lumpish mass of wool cardigan. He had a feeling that she didn't want to be looked at, so it *was* a kindness. So many women turned into sad sacks. It must have been the War . . . before the War his own mother had been a smasher . . . you could still see it in the family photograph album . . . her on the beach in her bathing-costume laughing in the summer of '39. She never got into a bathing-costume again after the War, though she could only have been forty-three. It had been the War, her giving all the good food to him and his father, saying she didn't feel hungry, she would just have a little bit of bread and butter . . .

He turned his eyes to her room instead. It was a room in two halves. In one half, dark, polished furniture was piled close, huddled like refugees in a cattle-truck. In the other half, two plain deal tables held a mass of filing-trays, typescript, Biros and a telephone.

Again, the woman seemed to sense the way his eyes were wandering, though she did not raise her eyes from writing firmly with a Biro in a pink book he knew to be a rent-book.

'I work for the BBC,' she said. 'I bring a lot of work home.'

'Are you on the telly?' he asked eagerly. Then bit his lip. Such a shabby creature could never get on the telly.

'Sound radio,' she said tightly, as if she sensed an insult. 'Only the overseas service. Talks on English culture. To places like West Africa.' She dismissed it all, with a flourish, as she handed him the rent-book. 'You've found your bathroom? Next floor down, on the left. I'm afraid it's not very convenient for you.'

He thought she had a nice voice; a posh, cultured, English voice; he was glad she had something left that was beautiful; as a sort of souvenir of her youth; like his aunt's legs.

He asked about the greatcoat and gas mask, very

haltingly. She just shrugged. 'Put 'em in the wardrobe, if they worry you.'

He was suddenly cross that she'd said 'worry' instead of 'bother' or 'annoy'. It made him sound like a hysterical kid, afraid of the dark. He instantly resolved to leave them where they were. He turned to go.

'Oh, one more thing,' she said, as he was half-way through the door. 'When you've unpacked your bags ... put them into the loft, will you? That's the door next to yours, at the head of the stairs. There is a light-switch, but you'll have to feel for it. Only, my cleaning woman doesn't like luggage lying around when she's dusting. Just makes her job more difficult, and cleaning women are hard to find these days.'

'Right,' he said, and left her.

The light-switch in the loft wasn't hard to find. The dim, bare bulb revealed roughly-laid boards, fading away into dimness and dust. There was already luggage stacked there; far better luggage than his poor fibre case and grip. Huge leather portmanteaus, with straps and torn and faded labels on the side. The Mena House Hotel, Gizeh, Egypt. The Grand Hotel, Biarritz. He stood there, feeling like a peasant; feeling that in his own little life, of which he had been so proud, nothing had ever happened. Even if he got his degree, a good degree, and a good job in teaching, and even eventually a headship or a training college lectureship, he could never afford to stay in the Grand Hotel, Biarritz. These people had a head start, and he could never catch up, even if he had a West End exhibition in Bond Street, and it was favourably reviewed in the *Observer* ...

He was just turning to go, in a flurry of self-disgust, when he saw the book, tucked in between a rafter and the roof proper, almost as if it had been wedged there to hold the roof in place.

And suddenly he was *very* nosy. He had been a book-child always. Whatever had come to him in the way of colour and excitement in his life had come from books. He could never leave a book unopened.

He reached out timidly and touched it. It seemed wedged pretty tight. Maybe it *was* holding some bit of the roof in place? He had an awful vision of tugging it out and something giving way, and slates falling and daylight showing through, and having to go and tell the woman downstairs what he'd done. There'd be no hiding what he'd done, because the rain would come, and the wetness would travel down through the house inexorably . . .

He was on the point of giving up, when the defiant book-child within him, the nosy child, gave one more tug, and the book was in his hand, thick with a sooty, grainy dust that almost bit at his fingers. And the smell was the choking smell of sulphur and soot and brimstone, the smell of London roof-tops, of a London far older than he was, that had him coughing beyond control. He held his handkerchief to his mouth so she would not hear him coughing all down through that dark house, and come up to find what he'd done.

But he realized with thankfulness that he'd done no damage to the roof. Nothing rattled and fell; no daylight showed. He switched off the light with a sooty hand, and closed the door leaving black fingerprints on it, and fled into his room. Gingerly he spread his handkerchief (his by now ruined white handkerchief that his mother had carefully washed for him and given him when he left home) on a part of the floor that was only polished board, where no harm could be done, and laid the book upon it.

Then he went downstairs to the bathroom and washed his hands, and fought a long battle to remove the wet, sooty fingerprints his hands were leaving everywhere. And then he came back and opened the book with newly-scrubbed, trembling fingers.

Something fell out, as it caught on his damp fingers. A square of thin cardboard, about ten by eight. It twisted as it fell, and lay face down. On the back was stamped,

Molloy Brothers, Photographers, 29 Bond Street

He turned it over and was lost.

It was a studio photograph of a girl; the sort that posh families get taken for *Country Life* when their daughter gets engaged to some bigwig.

It was obviously taken some time ago, for she was wearing that kind of shiny, satiny, clinging dress that they went in for in the 1930s. Cunning kind of dress; covered her up with complete modesty and yet showed to perfection what a marvellous figure she had. Only her long slender arms were bare. And her long, long neck.

It was the eyes that got him. Dark and huge. Sad. Infinitely romantic. Her lips were slightly parted in a smile, showing the tips of her top front teeth, in the way that was fashionable then.

He squatted motionless a long, long time, glorying in her fragile beauty; eating up every detail of her with his eyes. This was the sort of girl he'd always wanted: a lady, and yet with every evidence of being a woman too. He thought, when the photograph was taken, she must have been about his own age.

Finally, when he had temporarily looked his fill, he put her gently aside and looked at the book. It was some kind of business diary, the kind with a whole page given over to every day of the year.

And the year was 1940.

And on the very first page, what he knew must be her handwriting; elegant and spiky. He knew a little bit about graphology, as he knew a little bit about so many things. The tall ascenders meant she had high aspirations; the deep curling descenders meant she had a deeply sensuous nature. Or so the book on graphology he'd read had said.

And that first page was full; jam-packed with writing. And the next, and the next. So full of life; so long ago. All her inner life was spread before him, as if she lay naked on a bed. He could have her, all of her. Trembling, he read the first page.

'January 1st. First day of the year, and my birthday. I have reached the great age of 21. A third of my life is gone, and I have done nothing yet.

'John and Ros took me to the Café de Paris to celebrate. Champagne as usual. How sick I get of the never-ending champagne. What is there to celebrate? Only another useless year of my life is past. Oh, it was the year I got married to Ben, but that was all Ben's and my mother's and father's doing. As usual, I simply went along with the tide, the path of least resistance.

'Everyone was there at the café, the usual mob, working very hard at being jolly. Nearly everyone in uniform – but the kind of uniforms that keep them in London and give them endless time to go to the Café de Paris. Is nobody *fighting* this war? I am sure Hitler is not wasting time like this; he is plotting *something*. Chamberlain is useless, and so are the same old pack around him. The appeasers have gone into uniform, that's all. It is like a comic opera, a fancy dress ball. I am the worst of all, the fancy dress wife who has never even been to bed with her husband. Would I have ever married Ben, if I had *not* known he was going straight overseas from the church? If he gets killed, I shall be a fancy dress widow. Though he is not likely to die of anything in Egypt, except sunstroke.

'There was one man at the café who had really done something. An RAF squadron leader who has actually flown a bomber over Germany. Dropping leaflets. He was really quite amusing about it – says the Germans will never go short of lavatory paper. All his planes came home. He says the Germans could not find them in the dark. And none of the planes found their proper targets in the dark. It was like playing blind-man's buff – one of his planes had to land in the Orkneys they got so lost coming home – when they should have been in Lincolnshire . . .'

Harry came out of his dream of 1940 to hear a low, persistent tapping on his door. It had been so low, and so persistent that he only now realized it had been going on for some time before he'd noticed it; as if it was a normal part of the goings-on of the household. He looked round desperately for somewhere to hide the book and photograph, without his footsteps betraying him. Finally, in a panic, he shoved book and photo under the nearest rug on the floor. They made a square bump, but it couldn't be helped. Then he stood up, and called out breathlessly, 'Come in,' and suddenly didn't know what to do with his hands.

The woman entered; the muddy eyes behind her glasses everywhere but on his face. He could have sworn she noticed the square bump under the rug, but she made no comment.

'I thought you'd like to know that United Dairies deliver every day. Leave them a note of what you want in your empty bottle. They do eggs and butter and cream as well as milk. He calls on Friday evening for his money. And if you run out of bread on a Sunday morning, there's a convenient little Jewish baker just round the corner as you turn into the main road. And here's your front door key. Don't lose it, please. I'm not about very much in the evenings. I often have to work till midnight at Portland Place.' She gave him a timid, glancing swerve of her eyes. 'My name is Mrs Meggitt, as you will have gathered from your rent-book ... I'm going to work now. Good night.'

She closed the door behind her silently. He listened for her descending the stairs, but could hear nothing through the thick woodwork. It must be exciting, working for the BBC, and yet she filled him with nothing but dullness.

He put the front door key she had given him into his jacket pocket, then turned the key in the lock of his own door, and retrieved the diary, furtive as a spy now;

or a man going to a secret mistress. He sat at the narrow
table, and read; *her* photograph propped against a vase of
dried flowers watching him silently, sadly, yearningly.

'March 21st. First day of spring, officially, and the
weather for once came up to expectations. Wonderfully
warm, and daffodils out in St James's Park, where I
went to feed the ducks. Whoever goes short when the
rationing really starts, it won't be those ducks. They're
as fat as pigs, so fat they don't bother to fly any more.
And not just ducks, but lovers everywhere on the grass.
Quite shocking – one doesn't know where to look. The
men are mainly Polish and Canadian, in uniform, and
those uniforms seem to have an incredible effect on the
girls. Decorum is quite gone; the park keepers seem to
have lost hope of controlling them, and don't come
around any more. I was outraged while walking past
them, but as I came out through the park gates I felt
incredibly lonely. I got a wolf-whistle from some sol-
diers passing in a lorry which quite cheered me, though
it was a very half-hearted whistle by comparison with
the one that two WAAFs got a few yards further on.
Looking like a lady is going to have its disadvantages
in this war. I almost wish bombs would fall on London.
It would wake everybody up. It seemed so *real,* when
the sirens first went last September. I think I would
rather feel scared than feel nothing.'

He read on and on, enthralled. Until he suddenly felt
very cold and stiff, and looked at his watch and saw that
two hours had passed. He got up and stretched, and
tried to light the gas fire, but there was no gas. He
found the meter behind a little faded floral curtain under
a shelf, in the corner of the long room that served as a

kitchen, and stuffed in five shillings. But the fire once lit only made him feel colder, and he suddenly wanted the loo.

He hobbled downstairs, but then realized he didn't know exactly where the loo was. On the left, she'd said ... but he had to open two wrong doors before he found it. Two bedroom doors. And by the time he had found relief, he was seized by an overwhelming curiosity. He had few scruples, but he was not in the habit of invading other people's bedrooms when they weren't around. But he could have sworn that during his frantic search for relief he had seen, on the dressing-table of one of the bedrooms, a photograph of a girl ... a dark-haired, dark-eyed girl.

Yes, he had. He seized the neat silver frame and held it close. It was her; it *must* be her. Though she looked very different; smiling now, and looking upwards and hugging a fat, old, black Labrador.

Had this been *her* bedroom then? He stared around at the huge dark furniture, all highly polished, at the green satin bedcover, pulled tight as a board. It drove him to what he would never normally have done. He opened, furtively, drawers, wardrobes. They were still full of stuff. But the stink of moth-balls was over-powering, and the clothes were elderly women's clothes; thick grey stockings, wrinkled as an elephant's skin; long thick cotton directoire knickers; massive and dumpy fur coats. Some aunt's room. Some aunt who had kept a picture of her niece on the dressing-table. Of course people don't display photographs of themselves, stupid! Not on their own dressing-tables.

But by now he was committed to his sin; the bug had

truly bitten him. All sense departed. He plunged from room to room of the big house like a robber, a rapist. There *must* be more of her in this house.

Only once was he brought up short in his madness. By the room that was obviously Mrs Meggitt's; for spare, dumpy, shiny trousers hung in the wardrobe, and the drawers were full of drab, modern cardigans, and there was a spool of audio-tape with a loose end dangling on the dressing-table, and typescript for a talk on Indo-China on the bedside-table. He backed out hurriedly, as if caught red-handed in a burglary.

It was then that the strangeness struck him. Those trousers and jumpers, tape and typescript were the only things he'd found that belonged to *today*. Everything else could have come from ... the War, or before the War. It was almost as if he and Mrs Meggitt were camping out in the past.

He was heading downstairs to explore the ground floor when the front door suddenly opened, and Mrs Meggitt herself was there. Harry saw her sense his silent presence, look up ...

All he could do was continue down the stairs towards her. She looked at him enquiringly.

'I was thinking of going out for a bite to eat,' he said.

She looked at her watch. 'You've left it a bit late,' she said. 'Half-past eight. And it's raining.'

He just stood there, feeling a total fool. He couldn't see the expression on her face, against the dim light of the dusk outside. But she studied him a long time, then seemed to relent and said, 'There's a chip shop still open on the main road, if you like that sort of thing.' She said it with distaste. Then held out towards him the short, stubby thing that she had in her hand. He saw it was a woman's folding umbrella. 'You'd better take this.'

Once again, he fled from her. But she called, as he went through the front gate, 'Have you got your key?'

He was so glad that he could yell 'yes'.

On the way home, he got into a panic. He'd left his bedroom door standing wide open, and the book he'd stolen on the table wide open, with the photograph propped up. Suppose she went up there...?

He dumped her wet umbrella into the hall-stand, and ran up the stairs; like a madman. But the door was still just exactly as far open as he'd left it, and the book still lay, and the photograph was still propped up against the vase.

Of course, she might be the sneaky type, lying in wait for him to hang himself finally. But she didn't look the sneaky type; she looked the sort who lived inside her own head, in a world of her own.

He closed his door and locked it again, and sat at the table eating his fish and chips out of the newspaper, and still compulsively turning the pages of the big diary. Not reading it solidly, but skipping, now, looking for exciting bits. He was careful just to touch the edges of the pages; but in the end his hand slipped and he put a great big greasy thumb-print on one delicately-written page.

At first, he was horrified, and tried to rub it away with his hanky. But it wouldn't come off, and in the end he wasn't really sorry. He'd put his mark on her. He'd reached out from 1955 and put a mark on her in

1940. It seemed to him a sort of bridge between them, spanning time itself. He wondered where she was now, after all these years. Had the famous Ben come home and given her a brood of kids? She'd be fat and forty by now. Probably playing the memsahib in some corner of the dwindling British Empire. Or living in the country breeding dogs. He supposed Mrs Meggitt might know. But he wouldn't ask her; no fear. Didn't want to let the Meggitt's lifeless hands get on to his precious dream . . .

It was at that point that the diary suddenly ran out. October 9th, 1940. Frantically he searched the words of the last entry. 'October 8th. A long night. Bombing especially bad. The East End suffered again. Mrs Hewitt managed to filch five boxes of Mars bars for the van, and we had twenty gallons of coffee in the urns. Took a long time to get through; many roads blocked by debris or unexploded bombs. But the smiles we got from the Heavy Rescue men were reward enough. One gang had just dug out a little boy and his dog alive in Whitechapel, after twelve hours. Quite unharmed, and very brave, they said. He sang "Rule Britannia" for hours to guide them to where he was. Not much luck elsewhere. The body-sniffers were very pessimistic about their chances. Too busy to write more now. Will write later after I have slept.'

But after that, there was nothing. Just clean sheet after clean sheet, right till the end of the year.

It was then that Harry knew that she was dead. The saddest thing, he thought, was that he didn't even know her name.

*

He slept badly that night; the first time he had slept badly since the night before he sat Geography for Higher School Certificate, all of three years ago. In his dreams, he was back in his own little Blitz, on the north-east coast. He was seven years old again, down in the shelter, wanting the lav badly, while the Jerries chugged their broken note overhead, and the guns and rockets fired, bang, swoosh, with a noise that his gran said would waken the dead in Preston Cemetery.

Three times he started awake, and thought he could hear the siren going, or the all-clear; or the sky ringing, as if the guns had just stopped firing.

The last time, to convince himself it was only a dream, he got up and went to the window, and drew back the curtains. In his sleepy muddle, he even caught himself worrying about the black-out curtains. . . .

But outside, the night was clear and silent, except for that vague roar like distant surf that is London never sleeping. There were no searchlights or blinding flashes; only the dark orange glow over the West End that was merely neon street-lighting, not fires started. The moon was high and small-looking, very bright. Far off, he could just see the moonlight catching the curve of St Paul's dome.

Nothing.

And yet there was St Paul's, that had stood for three hundred years, and survived the Blitz. And below his window, on the bigger of the bomb-sites, was a static water-tank that had stood there since 1940. By daylight, you could see it was drained, so that kids could not drown in it, the bottom just littered with shallow puddles and half-bricks. But looking down at it now, in the shadows cast by the moon you could have almost sworn it was full again.

Bomber's moon, his dad used to call it, and oh how they used to fear it. Bomber's moon tonight. Suppose the all-clear had just gone, and the searchlights switched off? Suppose that orange glow over the West End *was* fires? There was nothing he could see outside his window that could prove it *wasn't* 1940 ... suddenly he scared himself, like he sometimes could. The artistic temperament, his mother called it. Said he had too much imagination. He pulled back inside the room, and looked for some object to comfort him. And saw the corporal's greatcoat and gas mask hanging on the back of his door. The identity card, a patch of white on the mantelpiece in the dim moonlight.

There were his clothes on the chair; but shirts and trousers and sweaters were much the same as they'd been in 1940 ...

Suddenly he was running for his jacket, hanging on the back of a chair. He dug in the inside pocket. There was his wallet, full of pound notes. But had pound notes been different in 1940?

Then he found his student union membership card: number 1174; dated October 1952. It was all rubbish, all just rubbish inside his head. He was safe, here in 1955, safe, safe, safe, with a bit of thin card.

But she, his lovely girl, was back in 1940. She smiled up at him from the table, her eyes just pools of dark in a patch of light. Had she been buried? She'd be a mouldering skeleton by now. Or had she been cremated by her sorrowing parents? Or burned in the Blitz? Or been blown to bits; small chunks of her picked from the telegraph wires by little innocent birds? He mourned for her with all his heart. And then perversely he wished again that time was elastic, and he could travel back and meet her, stand close, make love.

And then he told himself not to be a silly bugger, but to go back to bed and get some sleep, or he'd be bloody useless in life-modelling class tomorrow.

The next morning, he felt dozy, unreal, as he signed in at the porter's cubicle at the Slade. The place was milling with people he knew, back for the new term, but he only waved and kept his distance. Down in the basement, the senior sculpture class was busy stripping the sheets of plastic from their life-sized clay models, grumbling as they found parts of them too dry or too wet, after the long stretch of vacation. The clay models were nearly finished; this would be the last week of the pose. They echoed the shining creamy flesh of the living model on the rostrum with their dull lifeless greyness; one living model surrounded by all her dead imitation sisters . . .

He swung his own model round on its turntable, till it matched the angle of the living model, and his eye began the long check of details; angle of back of pelvis, jut of breasts, curve of thigh. Yes, he'd done some pretty good work, last term . . . then he went across to where the long sausages of soft new clay lay, fresh from the pug-mill, pulled off a handful, and stood poised to see where new dabs of clay were needed on the left upper arm of his own work.

But he couldn't settle. He was obsessed with the contrast between living flesh on the rostrum and the dead clay on the turntables. He knew the last thing he should be thinking of was the model's living flesh; that was a certain way to ruin his work. If the work was to progress, she must remain an abstract network of masses and thrusts, points of reference and measuring marks which he could measure with his clayey calipers. Think of her as a human being and emotion would come into it, and emotion, in this sculpture school at least, was certain death.

He struggled on manfully till three o'clock, and achieved nothing new. In a temper, he cut loose on one clay breast with a metal tool, digging away viciously, and nearly ruined something that he'd got right the previous term. And he had to struggle like hell, sweat running down into his eyes, to regain what he'd thrown away. When he had got it back, or *nearly* got it back, it was time for the model's last rest of the day. She slipped on a grubby, pink, satin dressing-gown, and went to talk to the student who everyone knew was her lover, gracefully standing with her weight on one leg, hand on hip. All round the room there were other girls, students. This one standing back from her work, both hands pushed up into her hair, with a gesture that unconsciously made the most of her breasts, usually hidden by the loose folds of her smock. Another girl lit up a fag and kept it in the corner of her mouth, squinting up her eyes against the smoke as she looked at her work. Usually he liked to watch the girls, unobserved. But today they seemed as dead and boring as the clay models. Only one girl was alive to him today; the girl in the diary. And she was dead.

He was seized by a terrible impulse to dash back to his lodgings and get on with reading the diary.

But something in him seemed to recognize a frightening temptation; so he resisted hard. Yet he knew it was dangerous for his work, to go on in this mood. So he went to the Students' Union for a cup of tea instead; then on to play table tennis with a bunch of cronies who he knew were busy failing their degrees. And they were going on to a screening of *Le Salaire de la Peur* starring Yves Montand, so he went with them.

Thus it was later, not earlier than usual, that he returned to his digs in Brangwyn Gardens.

Dusk was falling; but there were no lights on in the house. Mrs Meggitt must have gone to work already. But, perversely, as he took his key out of the front door, he called her name. Was he just making sure she was out? Or was he looking to contact some kind of friendly base camp before he ascended his dark pyramid?

When she did not reply, the whole dark house seemed to rustle awake. Seemed to become . . . sexually exciting. He climbed up past the white bear, expecting every second that something would leap at him out of some dark corner. Half dreading it, half wanting it.

But all he found, when he banged his light on, were his own things waiting for him as he'd left them that morning. But oddly fossilized and made strange by the lapse of time. Time, time, what a strange thing was time, he thought, as he cooked himself bangers and beans bought at the offie on the main road.

Then he settled on his bed with the diary.

'The news-vendors have an obscene new habit. On their billboards they are putting things like "116 for 32" as if they were advertising some Test Match. It is the number of planes the RAF have shot down, and how many *we* lost yesterday. And they shout the score with such ruthless cheerfulness. I almost slapped one who shoved his obscene paper in my face on the way down into the Piccadilly tube. I felt like shouting at him, "These aren't bats and balls you're shouting about, they were brave young men who were alive yesterday, laughing with their friends, and now they are dead, burnt to a cinder." I only just caught myself in time. But so many are dying up there in the sky while the world watches and makes a game of it, as if they were the ancient gladiators of Rome . . .'

At that point, Harry heard the front door bang open. He listened intently, to see if he could hear Mrs Meggitt's dreary footsteps through the thick wood of his door.

But to his amazement, he heard quite clearly that there was more than one person. A man's voice:

'I'll put these in your fridge to chill, Kath!'

Then a young woman's. 'Don't keep them there too long. I'm parched. I could drink a whole vineyard dry tonight.'

'And every other night, darling.' Another man's voice.

'God, you are a sot, Barbara.' Yet a third man's voice, light and clear.

'Who isn't these days, darling? Eat, drink and be merry . . .'

'Oh, God, she's going to talk about the bloody War again. It'll cost you a shilling, Barbara. Everybody who talks about the War puts a shilling in Kath's collecting box . . .'

'What's the box for, Kath?'

'Comforts for the troops.'

'The comforts the troops really need cost more than any shilling . . .'

'You offering, Megan?'

'She has already. It's her sole contribution to the War effort.'

Loud and prolonged laughter.

Harry simply couldn't believe what he was hearing. They sounded like a bunch of rep actors in a very bad play. Maybe they *were* in some play. In the West End? No, if they were in the West End, their play wouldn't have finished yet. By his watch it was only nine o'clock . . .

It was not to be borne. Harry had to find out exactly what was going on. If Mrs Meggitt had some secret life, a host of drunken friends, that was a fact so amazing . . .

He pushed the diary off his chest and jumped to his feet. Moved to open his door. The voices were clearer, louder, zooming up the dark stairwell.

'Kath? Kath? Glasses, for the love of Allah.'

'Cooooming . . .'

'Daft bugger can't see the hall-stand straight enough to hang up his coat.'

'If you'll shut that front door I can put a light on . . .'

Harry ran down one flight of stairs. In the dark. He did not wish to be seen. He ran down another, past the white bear, and down another.

'Corkscrew, Kath, corkscrew.'

'I always carry one in my gas mask case. *Voilà!*'

'Genius child. What would we do without you?'

Harry was poised on the first floor landing now.

Poised to dash down among them. He could always make the excuse that he was on his way for a bite to eat again. He plunged, as someone called, 'Dammit, don't spill it. I don't want to end up licking the carpet again tonight . . .'

The lower hall was in total darkness. The only light was a street-lamp outside, shining weakly in through the fanlight over the door. He gazed about him in bewilderment. Because he knew from the still, cold feel of the air, from the cold smell only of wax polish and dying flowers that there was nobody there, nor had there been anyone there for some time . . .

But unable to believe it, he ran to the front door and flung it open. Where had all the merry throng gone? They must be out in the street . . .

But under the unsympathetic orange glow of the street-lamps, there was only a solitary human figure, crossing the street towards him. She was carrying a bulging brief-case in one hand, and a carrier-bag in the other. It carried the logo of Victor Value's. She looked up at him, and her pebble glasses flashed in the lamp-light.

'Off for a bite to eat again, Mr Shaftoe? Are you sure your student grant can bear the expense?'

It wasn't just her sarcasm that made him suddenly hate her.

He lay in his bed, in his striped pyjamas, too full of bangers and beans, and the fish and chips he'd had to buy to support his alibi. He still quivered all over when he thought about the voices in the hall.

Of course, it might have just been a dream; brought

on by reading too much diary. He *had* come to with a start when he heard the voices, and he had been lying on his bed, with the diary heavy on his chest.

But the voices had gone on, after he'd got up. They had gone on right till he reached the last flight of stairs ... he couldn't *still* have been dreaming ... or was there such a thing as a waking dream, after you'd got up?

Or – and this was much more exciting – were there really ghosts? He had always wanted there to be ghosts. But he'd never seen one. The nearest he'd got was atmospheres in houses and churches. Every building had its atmosphere. He knew a chapel in Hereford cathedral where he literally seemed to go out of time, it felt so warm and safe and loving. His parents had found him there, after an hour, with what his father had described as a dozy grin on his face. And there was a church in York with an atmosphere so dreadful that you kept thinking the floor sloped down towards the middle, and the walls were leaning inwards, and the cross just looked like two old bits of wood nailed together. Even Methodist church halls had an atmosphere for Harry – an atmosphere of silly plays and dances, and ministers' fatuous announcements.

And those voices – they had seemed to suggest that the person who owned the house was called Kath. And he very much wanted Kath to be the girl in the picture – the name Kath would suit her. Kathleen, Catherine, Kathryn, like Kathryn Grayson, the film star ...

He listened carefully, hoping the voices would come again. But he only heard the sound of a late sports car outside, accelerating up Brangwyn Gardens with that freedom that came with empty streets after midnight.

Of course, it might be a sports car out of another time, a sports car from during the War. In the films, RAF fighter pilots always drove little sports cars. But a sports car was any time; not worth getting out of a warm bed for ...

Somewhere in this house, Kath must have lain alone in her warm bed ... in one of these unchanged bedrooms ... as Mrs Meggitt must be lying now. But he swerved away from thoughts of Mrs Meggitt, sleeping her pointless sleep as she lived her pointless life. What was the point of people's lives when they reached that age? What could she possibly be hoping for, looking forward to? She must be his parents' age. What did his parents have to look forward to? Well, himself and his older brother, Jack, and the way they were getting on in the world. And Jack's kids, Derek and Shaun. His own parents were busy being grandparents. But there was an aridness about Mrs Meggitt. You couldn't imagine her having children ... though there must have been a Mr Meggitt, poor sod ...

Anyway, he didn't want to think about Mrs Meggitt. He wanted to think about Kath, young and beautiful. And so deliciously vulnerable.

He rolled over and switched on his bedroom light, and picked the diary off the bedside rug, took the photograph out and propped it against the bedside lamp, and turned to what was already his favourite place in the diary.

'Air raids have an odd effect upon women. Quite different from the effect upon men. In the shelter, the men get very tensed up and restless. They are all ears. Was that a gun or a bomb? Here they come again ...

even when you strain your ears and can hear nothing. The men talk wildly about when are we going to bomb Berlin and give Adolf some of his own medicine? They discuss how Hitler should be punished after the War is over and he is in prison. It makes me quite sick, some of the things they say about punishing Hitler.

'The women are quite different. They grow flirty with the men around them, even when they are strangers. They nudge up to the men next to them on the wooden seats. If they are with their boy-friends, they want to cuddle and kiss, and more. Sometimes I don't know where to look. And I am talking about respectable women, housewives and young typists from the City. It is as if they were desperate for some warmth and love, even in the cannon's mouth, as Shakespeare would put it.

'I can't find it in my heart to blame them. I am just the same, especially during a raid when I am in this house and on my own. I have this fantasy of a man knocking at my door to get in to safety during a raid. Perhaps he is slightly injured. I lie him down on the bed in the cellar and then ... I don't know what I should do if a real man were ever to knock ... I'd probably come to my senses and be quite prim. Like I always become when the raid is over, and the all-clear goes. I seem to be two people. Two sisters inside the same skin ...'

Harry put the diary down, turned out the light, and fell into his own fantasy. And finally slept. His last thought was of the nature of time. Of the fifteen years that lay between himself and the beautiful lonely Catherine like a massive impenetrable pad of grey insulation material, the consistency of the ex-army blankets on his bed. If only he had been the one to knock on her door! But he'd only been six then, a little boy in short trousers that Mam had made for him; two hundred miles away on the north-east coast.

Next evening, he had no sooner put his key into the lock of number eleven Brangwyn Gardens than the thought hit him – like an electric shock that made the world go black before his eyes, and his knees tremble.

He could go and look for the cellar with the bed in it.

But first he must make sure that Mrs Meggitt was not at home. He was so much wanting her not to be that he got another shock when she called 'come in' in response to his knock on her door. He had to open the door, knowing he hadn't a thought in his head about what he was going to say to her. She did not look up from where she sat by the old gas fire, warming her shabby slacks at the tiny warmth, a typescript on her knee.

'Yes, Mr Shaftoe?' She did not bother to look up at him even now, or stop reading the script.

'I got a bit of a fright last night,' he said, lamely. 'I was lying on my bed when I thought I heard voices down here in the hall. A lot of people, having a sort of party. But when I came down, there was nobody there.'

'What time was this?' She still went on reading, and her voice was very bored.

'Just before I met you. That was why I opened the front door.'

'I thought you said you were going out for a bite to eat?'

'That as well.' She was starting to make him feel a proper fool.

'Well, I can explain about the voices. It's living in a terrace that does it. Voices echo off the housefronts opposite. I often think I hear a taxi pulling up outside; but when I look, it's thirty yards away down the street.'

He almost felt she was a fellow human being for a moment; he almost pitied her. Expecting someone coming in a taxi who never came. Then she said,

'Is there anything else?' in a dismissive voice, and he half-hated her again. So he said, half-jokingly, but meaning to shake her,

'I thought the house was haunted for a minute.'

She made a squiggle on the typescript with the Biro in her hand; like a severe schoolmistress correcting an essay, and said,

'You don't believe in that kind of nonsense, do you?'

'Places have atmospheres,' he said defiantly.

'*What* places?'

'Old churches.'

'You mean they have pretty, old, stained-glass windows, and smell of incense and woodworm-killer?'

'It's more than that.' His voice rose to an indignant squeak.

'You obviously have the artistic temperament, Mr Shaftoe.'

'This house has got an atmosphere.'

'You mean it's full of old unsellable junk?' She sounded as if she really hated the house. As if she was forced to live there against her will.

'Good night,' he said, and walked out stiffly, closing the door with a precise and angry click.

He left his own door open, and listened for the bang of the front door as she went to work.

She went about seven.

Immediately, he was tiptoeing downstairs; only wary, in case she had forgotten something and came back for it.

He found the door and steps down to the basement easily enough; the porcelain and brass light-switch resisted his hand, then went down with an almighty click.

He was in a huge dim kitchen, with stone flags, huge tables, and massive black pans on shelves. A big schoolhouse clock on the wall, stopped at ten to four, probably for ever. Black-beetles scurried away from under his feet. What on earth did black-bettles find to live on, he wondered. This place obviously hadn't been cooked in for years.

There was a black warden's helmet, with a white 'W' painted on it, hanging on the back of a further door. It was like a friendly signpost, saying he was on the right track.

But the room beyond was only a scullery, with two huge Belfast sinks and nothing else.

Except that through its dusty window, across the area with its dustbins, he could see another door. And after a tussle with the rusty outside lock, it was there he found it. The cellar. It had once been the coal-cellar, but somebody had painted the arch of London brick with thick coats of whitewash, some of which had flaked off, to reveal the coal-ingrained brick beneath. It lay under the roadway; a heavy brick arch with three feet of road-surfacing above it. It would have been a good air raid shelter, against anything but a direct hit; far safer than the basement of the house.

And in it, one on each side, two narrow beds, made up with the same grey Army blankets as he had himself. One bed was unused, as flat as a board. The other had been lain on; there was the impression of a body lying on its back. There was the dent of a head in the thin-striped pillow, minus any pillowcases.

From the width of the depression around the hips, it must have been a woman. He could clearly see the twin impressions left by the buttocks. He thrust his nose at the depression in the pillow, like an avid dog. Was there, under the pervading dry mustiness, a hint of some perfume, rather sweet and old-fashioned and innocent? Lily of the Valley, like his mother had used? It seemed impossible, after all those years; it *all* seemed impossible after all those years. Yet, if she had lain down on top of this bed, during a raid, and nobody else had ever come again, why *should* it be impossible? How else could it have been?

He straightened up, and looked around. There was a blue Thermos flask, on the rackety little table beside the bed. He unscrewed it; it was empty and smelt foul, as empty Thermos flasks always do. But he thought it might once have held weak coffee, with something alcoholic in it. Something to keep up her courage. And there was a book too, a little leather-bound black book with golden edges that winked at him dimly as he lifted it, like a goldfish swimming in murky water. A Bible.

With a paper bookmark, marking the place of the 23rd Psalm.

And the name in the front of the Bible was Catherine Winslow. To Catherine from her loving Grandmother, on the occasion of her confirmation, May 1st 1931.

It was so pathetic. The coffee and alcohol to keep up her courage; the Bible to keep her safe. The Lord is my Shepherd, I shall not want.

And she had been dead for fifteen years.

He backed away, as if from some holy shrine, feeling ashamed at what visions he had had of her, what fantasies. He had some feelings of piety still left in him, in spite of a student dalliance with atheism and Marxism. Piety learnt saying his prayers long ago at his mother's knee, as a four-year-old.

His mother would still say that Catherine Winslow was with the angels now. And yet Catherine Winslow had wanted to take a man down to that shelter and ...

In a thorough muddle, he ran back upstairs to his room.

Once there, he paced about restlessly. He felt so close to her. But he wanted to be closer. Somewhere in this house, in which nothing had changed for fifteen years, *must* be her bedroom, her personal things. He had to find it. He wanted to run his hands over everything.

He looked at his watch. It was only half-past seven. Mrs Meggitt had only been gone half an hour. He was safe enough.

And so he went down through the house, bursting into room after room like an invader. Most of the rooms, though fully furnished, were desolate. A clear top to the dressing-table; empty drawers. Guest bed-rooms.

It was two floors down that he found it. The little bookcase gave it away. Its copies of *Wind in the Willows* and *The House at Pooh Corner* still had her name in them.

CATHERINE WINSLOW
ELEVEN BRANGWYN GARDENS
LONDON
THE WORLD
THE SOLAR SYSTEM
THE UNIVERSE

But it was the things she'd had when she grew older ... Not just Vera Brittain's *Testament of Youth* but the grown-up powder compact, still with its powder-puff and powder inside. And the scent-spray with its little green-rubber bulb. And the wardrobe full of long dresses and curiously-pointed shoes. And the chest of drawers with its foaming, lacy mass of underwear, amongst which snuggled little sachets of dried lavender that still gave off a faint, sweet smell.

He even dared disturb the rigidly-made double bed. And under the bolster, neatly folded, he found her white night-dress.

It was then he thought he heard the front door close quietly downstairs. He froze in horror. He became a child of five again, caught out in some dreadful sin. If Mrs Meggitt found him here, he would be thrown out forthwith. It was beyond bearing. He broke out in a cold sweat, wave after wave of sweat, staring at the open door and waiting to be discovered.

But he waited a long time, and nothing happened.

No further sound came up the stairs; and by this time he knew what sounds to expect from Mrs Meggitt. The clack of her black lace-up shoes on the cold tiles of the hall; the clang of the kettle in the little place out back, which she now used as a kitchen.

He felt an overwhelming thankfulness; a craven thankfulness such as he had never felt in his life before. He thought he had been let off his sin. He glanced around the room, to make sure that he'd left nothing disturbed. He saw his palm-print in the light dust that lay on the dressing-table, and took out his handkerchief and polished the shiny surface until every touch of dust was gone. Then he closed the door so softly behind him, flinching at the slight click the lock gave. Then a quick glance round the two landings to make sure that every other door was shut, as he'd found it, and he plunged down to the ground floor, to seek out the worst. He *had* to know if Mrs Meggitt was in the house; there was no way he could get back to normal till he knew.

He tapped on her door, and got no answer, though when he tried the handle, the door was locked. Did that mean she didn't trust him; that she knew what he got up to when she was out? To drive away this doubt, he began to call her name.

'Mrs Meggitt? Mrs Meggitt?' Soon, as his confidence grew that she was out of the house, his voice soared into a shout.

It was a long time before he felt thoroughly safe. When he finally did, he went slowly and heavily upstairs; he felt worn out. He flung himself down, reached for the diary from under his bed, and held it, closed, on his chest. But he was too weary even to look at it.

He must have dozed off. It was the song that wakened him. It was a song he knew well, from the War.

> 'That certain night, the night we met
> There was magic abroad in the air
> There were angels dining at the Ritz
> And a nightingale sang in Berkeley Square.'

He looked dazedly at his watch. Only ten to nine. Time seemed to be playing funny tricks tonight. And it was a funny time to hear that song. You still heard it played sometimes on record-request programmes; but most record-request programmes were in the mornings, he was sure . . .

He lay still, heard it through till the end. Was just dozing off when it started up all over again. It must be a record. It *was* a record, because he heard it slow and slur, and then speed up again, as someone rewound the handle. Not a modern electric record-player, then, but an old wind-up gramophone. That didn't sound like Mrs Meggitt, with her modern tape recorders . . .

He shot upright, tingling all over. Was it . . .

He tiptoed to the door in his stockinged feet, and stepped out on to the landing, and heard the record start up a third time. The wild thought came that *she*, Catherine, knew what he had been doing, searching for her room, handling her night-dress. And that she was not displeased with him. Was actually calling him.

Softly he crept downstairs, through the scratchy waves of music.

On the first floor landing, the music simply stopped. In mid-record. No running-down of the gramophone;

no click of the needle being lifted off. Just silence, like a blanket. And the solidness of the silence told him, without hope, that it would not start again.

He felt all the dark excitement go out of him in a wave. Making him feel quite hopeless. He sat down in the middle of the last flight of stairs with his head in his hands, and groaned aloud to himself.

A door swung open downstairs. Mrs Meggitt's door. He sensed a beam of light fall on him, glimmering through his closed eyelids.

Mrs Meggitt's cross voice floated up to him:

'Mr Shaftoe? Is that you? Mr Shaftoe, are you all right? Was that you groaning? Are you *ill*?'

He got up shakily and said, 'I stubbed my toe on the banister. It hurts.'

'I'm not surprised, if you insist on wandering around without shoes. Was there something you wanted? You surely weren't going out for a bite to eat without *shoes* on?'

'No ... I ... I thought I heard you playing a record, over and over. It's a favourite of mine. I haven't heard it for years. From the War. It's called "A Nightingale Sang in Berkeley Square".'

'Certainly not. I'd just got the television on, in time for the news.'

And now he could hear the TV news theme tune, the familiar, bouncy, official tones of the news-reader's voice. Something about the Suez Canal ...

'Sorry,' he said, and turned to go.

He heard her sigh with exasperation as he went.

He was sitting in a daze on his bed, holding the diary,

when he remembered he had seen something about 'A Nightingale Sang in Berkeley Square' in it. Not in a part he'd read properly. He'd just noted it in passing, because she had put it inside double inverted commas, instead of single inverted commas, which was the correct thing to do. While he was skimming through, the first time he'd opened the diary, he'd noticed it. He'd sneered a bit, and passed on.

Now he searched for it desperately, so that he was a long time in finding it. But he found it in the end.

'February 11th. Last week, I got a record of "A Nightingale Sang in Berkeley Square". Sung by Judy Campbell. From the West End show *New Faces*. It is all the rage at the moment, so with the shortages and all, I was very lucky to get it. I took it home and played it and played it. I'm afraid I wept, because it reminded me of London in happier times. Well, if I'm to be honest, not just that. It is so romantic. I thought it would make me think of poor Ben, out in Egypt. But it didn't. It made me want some other man, whose face I can't even see – a man who lives only in my mind, a man who will sweep me off my feet like poor Ben never did. A dark, secret man, with whom I will do dark, secret things. I sometimes think I am going crazy. But it is just the War. London is full of men, and, in the black-out, dark, secret things going on in dark, secret places. All the husbands and wives apart and alone; it is as if some Great Being has shuffled the pack of cards all over again, and the game can be won by anyone who dares to play it. But I don't dare to play it. The worst poor little innocent me can do is to change into my virginal nightdress and play my record over and over again and *wish*. While that mood is on me, I seem to go out of time altogether. Well, not tonight. Tonight I will drink cocoa, and go to bed early and sleep sound.'

It was lying in bed that night that the whole thing seemed to become clear to him; on the very verge of sleep. As things so often do.

She was still in the house.

She had never found her lover.

She was calling to *him*.

But she was like a bird, timid, shy.

And yet she wanted him so *much*.

And Mrs Meggitt was her enemy. Her clumsy un-witting earth-bound enemy, who didn't even know she existed. Where Mrs Meggitt was, she could never come.

'Can you really come? I can't come to you, I don't know how. Is there really a way? I want you so *much*. Find a way, *please*,' he said to her, in his mind.

And then, still wishing, still muddled, he was asleep.

It was the sound of the siren that wakened him. He lay helpless, sweating. Is it 1940? Should he get up and rush to the shelter? He had a terrible impulse to, when he heard the sound of bombers, when the cracks of the guns echoed through the house.

But he only reached out to his bedside-table, and found the photo and the diary. That somehow meant he was safe; still in 1955. In any case, even in 1940, this house was never hit by a bomb, his coward self assured him.

More than that, he must be *passive*. He could not find

his way to her. He was alive. Alive made you clumsy. When he rushed at her, she vanished. She must come to him. She would know how. Because she was dead.

Were those soft footsteps outside his door? How could he tell, above the noise of the guns? Was she waiting there, listening too, breathing softly, trembling? He strained his ears. Would she knock?

A flashing at the curtains of his windows made him swing his head. The searchlights . . . ? Then the flashings were lost in a steady brilliant blue glare that he remembered. Incendiary bombs.

There was a rattle on the roof, down the slates into the gutter. God, that was an incendiary too. On the house. How well he knew the sound. He must deal with it, before it set the house on fire . . .

But no, he must lie passive. Or it would all vanish away . . .

He sniffed. Was that the smell of Lily of the Valley?

And then he thought of the cumbrous form of Mrs Meggitt lying in her bed downstairs. Where was she in all this, hearing nothing, seeing nothing, snoring on?

As if he had broken some spell, there was silence in the house.

Stillness. Nothing.

He switched his bedside light on then. Checked his watch. Half-past two. Went to the window, pulled back the curtains, opened the window.

Nothing but the dim orange glow over the West End. Nothing but the distant growl of London never sleeping. Sounding almost like waves breaking on a distant shore.

But he still looked into the guttering, where the rattling sound had ended up.

His skin crept. There was something there. Something slim and long and light-coloured, about the size of a big torch. If he stretched out his hand, he could touch it, grasp the round coolness of it.

He knew what it was before he drew it in and looked at it.

A German incendiary bomb of 1940, with the green tail-fin still attached, and the yellow German markings on the pale, shining side.

She had done what he asked.

She had breached time itself.

With a sudden moan of fear and revulsion, he shoved it back where it had come from, and slammed the window, and drew the curtains and went and huddled by his bedside light.

Tomorrow, he told himself over and over again, he would pack his bags and leave. But he had to tell himself that a long time, before he finally slept.

In the morning, grinning at him, jeering at him, the bomb was still in the gutter. He had no heart to touch it. Maybe, he told himself, it had been lodged all these years behind some chimney-stack and the wind had finally dislodged it. Maybe, he told himself, the whole thing had just been a nightmare.

But a bloody morbid nightmare. Not a nightmare he would ever want to have again. And he'd bloody asked for it, rummaging through the underclothes of a woman who'd been dead fifteen years. He felt a terrible revulsion at all the things he had done, a deep uncleanness. He must have been *mad*!

It was all the fault of the house. It was all Mrs Meggitt's fault, the morbid old bitch, keeping the place like some sodding museum. Well, he'd have no more of it. He would pack his bags and go today. This very morning. He was sure his mate Timmy Waters would let him sleep on his floor for a couple of nights, while he found somewhere else to rent.

He packed his bags, right down to the tea and sugar packets on the little work-surface. Then he went downstairs to tell her. He knocked on her door, and heard her footsteps inside. The door opened.

'Ah, Mr Shaftoe. I'm glad you knocked. I wanted a word. I've just had a summons to dash up to Edinburgh for a couple of nights – talks on Scottish country life for the Hong Kong programme ... I'm relying on you to keep an eye on the house and feed my cat. I hope you don't mind. I'd be so grateful.'

All he could think of to say was, 'I didn't know you had a cat.'

'She keeps to the kitchen. It's better that way, than having her coming into the house. She's getting rather old and frail, and her bladder's not very reliable any more, I'm afraid. If you'll come through, I'll show you where things are kept.'

He followed her through, trying all the time to frame the words that would get him off the hook and give him a chance to run.

But she never seemed to stop discussing arrangements for the cat. And her calm assumption that he would help was a wall he could not climb. What made it worse was that the cat was a sweet-natured, rather lovely, old, grey tabby, that rubbed her head against his hand trustingly.

'Right, that's settled then. I must be off, I've a train to catch. The 9.15 from King's Cross. See you Friday!'

As if by magic, she hoisted what looked like a portable tape recorder with a strap on to her shoulder, from where it had been lying just inside her room door; snatched up a holdall from beside it, and was out of the front door before he could open his mouth.

The door slammed behind her.

In the darkness of the hall, he almost felt the house rustle into life. Mrs Meggitt had gone; the sensible old cork had come out of the bottle; the lid of Pandora's Box had been opened with a vengeance now.

He ran; he ran all the way upstairs, and all the way down again; with the great encumbering weight of his luggage, he almost tripped and fell headlong. Twice. Steady, Shaftoe, steady! You don't want to be lying here in the dark for two days, with a broken leg.

He did not stop until he reached a Joe Lyons' tea-shop, half a mile along the main road. It was starting to rain heavily, and he'd packed his mack, so he slipped inside. He sat miserably over a cup of tea and a bit of custard-tart, worrying about the cat.

Hell, he told himself, there's no chance of it starving to death in two days. It'll survive.

But it'll need something to drink . . .

It can go outside and drink from puddles . . .

But it might get wet and die of pneumonia. It was old, for God's sake . . .

Well, it was too late to worry now.

Or was it? He felt for his house key, and it was still in his jacket pocket.

And he hadn't left Mrs Meggitt any kind of note. She might get worried, report him missing to the police. Oh, shit, what a *mess*!

He would write her a letter from Timmy Waters' place, and enclose the key, wrapped up in tissue paper.

But the letter mightn't get there before Friday ...

The rain came down heavier, beading the big plate-glass window with trickling drops, and making it steam up inside. Buses and cars passed, with their lights on, making a great hissing with their tyres on the wet mirror-black street. Women kept on coming into the tea-shop, shaking collapsed umbrellas, peeling off soaking headscarves from their damp hair. The air filled with the smell of wet people. God, it was getting so *sordid*; somewhere towards the back of the shop, a child began to cry, making his nerve-ends curl up like it always did.

Suddenly, he hated the humdrumness of the world. But he supposed it served him right. He had run away from the supernatural; what could he have left except the ordinary? Rainy days and red, plastic table-tops, fat, ugly, middle-aged women and squalling brats?

When he might have stayed behind at Brangwyn Gardens and learnt the truth; about so many things.

'Anybody sitting here?' It was a little thin old cockney in a cap, with a grey-green drip on the end of his nose. He settled, sniffing as regularly as the tick of the grandfather clock at Brangwyn Gardens, and took out a racing paper, and began mumbling horses' names to himself out loud.

So that was how you ended up in the ordinary world ...

Suddenly he had a vision of Catherine's photograph, still propped up against his bedside lamp at Brangwyn Gardens. Beautiful, beautiful virginal Catherine, still waiting for him.

Suddenly he was on his feet, hauling his luggage from under the old cockney's legs. ''Scuse me.'

The cockney's bleary old eyes watched him go. 'Funny sort of feller,' he said, to no one in particular. 'Must be in love or somefink.'

Harry walked fast through the easing rain, eager to meet his fate.

But fate takes its time. The house at Brangwyn Gardens was as quiet as any other empty house. He thought he smelt a trace of Lily of the Valley on the first landing; caught himself sniffing for it almost like an animal; but sniff as he could, it did not come again.

He spent a lot of the day in Mrs Meggitt's kitchen, talking to the cat, rubbing her ears, trying to get her to play with a spill of paper. But after he'd fed her at six o'clock, as per instructions, the sun came out in the wilderness of a garden, and with a flip of the cat-flap, she abandoned him. And he knew it was time to be with Catherine upstairs.

Through the big dormer window, the sunset was building up magnificently. The view of St Paul's dome, washed free of smoke by the rain, had never been more detailed and magnificent. He felt he could almost reach out and touch it.

'Red sky at night, shepherd's delight,' he said to no

one in particular. He hadn't said it since he was a little kid, watching the sunset on Tyneside, waiting for night to come and the raid to start.

Then he settled for a last time to Catherine's diary. Determined to read every bit of it.

'September 1st. They have let me join the WVS. I am the youngest member by at least forty years. They are a magnificent body of women; all upper class; pure Home Counties. No doubt their dogs are missing them back home. *Never* caught without their hats, however bad the bombing gets. I am co-driver of a van, with Mrs Hewitt. Our job is to run refreshments to the Heavy Rescue gangs in the East End. The tea-wagon always gets through! I feel some use at last!

'October 5th. I have found my dark and dangerous man at last. I was off duty last night, and went down to the Gluepot, hoping to catch Lou and Michael in their usual snug by the bar. No such luck, but place very crowded. Saw this Polish corporal looking at me through the bar mirror. Very dark; long, greasy hair under his forage-cap, moustache. Not at all the usual kind of corporal. He just kept staring at me, in the most disconcerting sort of way. I tried to ignore him, but my eyes kept on drifting back to him. Very handsome in a Polish sort of way – high cheek-bones. Finally, he came across and asked if he could buy me a drink. I was amazed. He spoke excellent cultured English. Also French and German, as far as I could make out. I asked him what he was doing for the War Effort, but he clammed up and wouldn't tell me. Very hush-hush, I gather. But he suddenly said, "I have a week's leave and I know no one." And so I asked him to come home and stay with me. Just like that. I amazed myself. But why shouldn't I too have my dark and dangerous man? I have put him in the attic. I can hear his footsteps overhead as I write. What is going to become of me? I don't think I really care, so long as it's dark and dangerous. The way the war is going, we might all be dead in a month anyway.'

Harry suddenly switched the bedside light on. It was getting too dark to read. The bedside lamp made the room suddenly darker. But he could still see the corporal's stripes on the greatcoat that was hanging on the back of his door.

And the thought came to him. Did she die in the East End raids, as he'd always thought? Or had she died in this house? And not from a bomb?

He read on, but there was nothing more about the Polish corporal. Just entries like, 'Heavy raid. Did not get home till seven.' Seven at night, or seven in the morning? Harry didn't even know that. It was as if she had become too busy to write.

After he had finished the diary, he didn't know what to do with himself. He had no inclination to read anything else.

What would the Polish corporal have done? Got washed? Got into his pyjamas? Lounged smoking on his bed? Listened for sounds of the woman downstairs? Both of them listening, straining their ears.

For the siren, for the bombers, for death coming?

For a foot on the stair, an opening door, love coming?

The two of them held together by the long strands of listening, through the dark silent house.

It came to Harry then that he must play his part too.

Get washed, get into his pyjamas, lounge on the bed.

There was a strong waft of Lily of the Valley, as he went into the bathroom.

She was pleased with him. He was doing it right.

He got into pyjamas and dressing-gown and lay on his bed listening. But he had almost fallen into a stupor when he heard it ... The gramophone start up.

'That certain night, the night we met
There was magic abroad in the air
There were angels dining at the Ritz
And a nightingale sang in Berkeley Square.'

On and on it played. Even after, in the far distance, there came the sound of the siren. On and on till surely the Polish corporal would answer it, come down to find out what was happening?

Harry got up and moved towards his door. Then a distant sound of aircraft engines, of gun-fire, made him look nervously towards his two windows.

It worried him that the black-out curtains weren't drawn. It made the Blitz-kid in him feel exposed, insecure. He reached behind the faded floral curtains and drew the stiff, hard, black folds. And felt on the back of his hand the clinging of cobwebs, the fall of small, cold, dry, insect bodies.

It was hard to get them to draw together, the curtains. They were so old, so set. But he managed it at last.

And then, from downstairs, he heard the needle snatched off the record. So hard and savagely that it screeched like a wild thing.

As if somebody, suddenly, had made up their mind ...

He tiptoed to the door of his room, after switching off his own light. Went and peered over the banister rail, down into the well of darkness below.

There was not total darkness. There was one thin shaft of dim light, prominent as a searchlight in the dark.

It came from the partly-open door of Catherine's bedroom.

He waited, motionless, trying to control his harsh breathing. His tongue explored the roof of his mouth; it was as dry as leather. He licked it back to moistness.

And then he heard the stair creak. Near the bottom. Then creak again, on the second flight. Was it a real creak, or the ghost of a creak?

And then something dimly white swam into view, far below. Coming up the stairs. As it grew nearer the light from her door, a smaller white patch became visible on the handrail, moving. A hand.

Then below, the movement that could only be bare white feet.

The thing paused, at the patch of light that was her door. Now he saw clearly the night-dress, the clinging satiny night-dress; the bare pale arms, the long neck, the cascading fall of dark, black hair. But still not her face.

And then she turned and looked up at him. And he would have known those dark, tragic pools of eyes anywhere.

And as he clung to the banister rail, swaying; as his whole universe swayed and swung around him, she smiled, with an upward smile.

Still he could not move. His body refused to move. His mind said enough, you have seen enough. This is all you need.

But it was not all she needed. For she raised a white hand and beckoned.

And under him, his bare feet began to move. Slowly, slowly, down two whole flights on the soft, silent carpet, while in the distance the guns rumbled; and her eyes held him, across the dark depths of the stairwell.

He halted, a few feet from her. He knew beyond doubt it was Catherine. But what *sort* of Catherine?

She smiled again, a friendly understanding sort of smile, and yet an executioner's smile too. A sympathetic executioner's smile. And then her hand reached out to take his . . .

Would it be empty air, or cold bone? Whatever it was, he had to take it.

But it was neither empty air, nor cold bone. A real girl's hand, solid, if rather thin and cold.

Beyond her, he saw the single candle on her mantelpiece, that lit her room with a dim, golden light. He saw the satin bed, no longer rigid as a board, but opened and welcoming, with big pillows and white sheets.

We have crossed time itself, he thought; and as she drew him in, he seemed to walk among the stars, as well as the fretful guns.

He swam back towards consciousness, groping for memories of the night. The terrible times when she had clung to him, and whispered of dreadful, unbelievable things; of buses fallen into holes in the earth; of babies split wide open like a burst pillow; of shelters where everyone sat dead, without a mark on them. Whispered till the whisper grew towards a scream, and he screwed up his bare legs in terror, and fought to disentangle his wet body from her strangling arms, and failed.

And the other times, when she needed him and opened herself to him and it was a ride of terror and glory with the broken drone of German bombers passing overhead, and the shrapnel rattling on the roof.

I have known it, he thought, and survived. For the rumpled sheets were warm under him, and the dim light of morning was starting to filter through his closed eyes, and he knew the bed was empty of her at last.

He kept his eyes shut a long time, because now it was gone, he wanted to recapture and store every moment of it. He had done it and survived; a journey through time itself.

As his granny had always said, love was stronger than the grave.

But he had to open his eyes at last; his bladder was full to bursting.

He opened his eyes, and Mrs Meggitt was sitting on a chair drawn up across from the bed, looking at him through her pebble spectacles, wearing her shiny baggy slacks, thick pilled grey cardigan, and lace-up shoes.

Glory turned to panic. He was a little boy caught out; tossed and naked in a sacred memorial of a bed. All he could think of to say was, 'I thought you were in Scotland.'

It was not even the beginnings of an excuse. He

expected her to start to rave and scream at him, to throw him out into the street, naked as he was, to write and complain to the Lodgings Officer, to get him thrown out of the university ... but she simply said, 'I came back early.'

'I'm sorry ...' he started feebly.

'There is no need to explain,' she said, not angry; no emotion at all, really. Then she bent down and picked something off the floor, and showed it to him.

Through bleary eyes, he saw it was the incendiary bomb; the German incendiary bomb he had left out on the guttering.

He scanned her face, incredulous. But her muddy eyes swam away from him, behind the thick pebble lenses. And the silence went on and on.

Finally, he took a deep breath and said, 'You *know*. You know it *all*.'

'Yes,' she said. 'I know it all.'

Suddenly, he understood. She was ... the humble, faithful acolyte, the priestess of this shrine. Who kept it and guarded it selflessly, so that, in her good time, the dead goddess could come. She was the one who cleared up afterwards.

Instead of feeling ashamed, he suddenly felt proud. She knew what he had done; she knew of his wild ride through time. He could discuss it with her. She was the only person in the world he could ever discuss it with. Suddenly he felt a little glow of affection towards her, poor old thing.

'Was she your daughter?'

A slight, bitter smile crossed the woman's pale, life-less lips. She shook her head, and he knew he had said something hurtful. He was eager to make amends. 'Your younger sister?'

Another wry shake of the head.

'Your . . . friend?'

'No,' she said, and for once her eyes did not swim away behind her pebble glasses. 'She was *me*!'

And at once, for some reason, he knew she was mad. He was fastened up, naked, with a revolting madwoman.

'You don't believe me, do you?' She smiled, a quite horrible smile.

'No,' he said stoutly, pulling up the bedclothes around his nakedness.

'How old do you think I am then?'

'Fifty-five,' he said savagely. 'Sixty!'

'And how old would . . . *she* have been. If she'd lived?'

He did not answer.

She reached up slowly, and undid the tatty old headscarf.

A cascade of dark, lovely hair tumbled down. Hair that he *knew*. Young, young, lovely hair, on an old, old face.

She began to undo the belt of the old pilled cardigan.

The long neck, the night-dress . . . the long, smooth, bare arms. And the pebbled glasses.

And then with a gesture, the pebbled glasses went. For a moment, the face was still set in the rigid, hard lines of a landlady.

And then she smiled the smile of last night.

He covered up his eyes and moaned, 'No, no, no.'

Without taking his hands away from his face, he said feebly, 'The incendiary bomb . . .'

'I've had it since the War, Harry. Souvenir. I stuck it into the gutter while you were out, and you never noticed it, till I went out into the garden and threw a stone on the roof, that night.'

'The guns, the sirens, the bombers.'

She laughed, a low, mad laugh. 'They have a full archive of tape recordings, at the BBC. I have loud-speakers, here and there.'

'The perfume!' he shouted defiantly.

'A little pad of cotton wool, under the carpet. Where you will tread on it.'

'The diary . . .'

'The diary is real. I wrote it, in 1940. The first student I had found it. That's what started it all. Young men are so in love, with love and death.'

'But *why*?' He glared at her, full of rage now.

Her face changed, from expression to expression, so that first she looked like a younger, handsomer Mrs Meggitt, and then she looked like a worn, weary Catherine; and then her face lit up with memory, so she just looked like real Catherine, ghostly Catherine. That was worst of all.

'My first dark and dangerous man . . . I suppose he did kill me really. He was wonderful for a week, but he never came back.'

'Was . . . was he killed in action?'

'I don't know. I never even knew his name.'

'What about . . . Ben?'

'Ben never came back either. Killed in Egypt.'

'And ever since . . .'

'Sometimes the tricks worked; sometimes they didn't.' She laughed to herself. 'I got pretty clever at it.'

'But why did you have to? You're . . .' He was going to say, 'A handsome woman. Thirty-six years old.' Which she was, even by daylight. And then he watched the expressions playing across her face, one after the other. And young as he was, he despaired.

Instead, as something to say, he said lightly, 'So the house wasn't haunted after all, then?'

She looked at him straight for a moment; looking a handsome thirty-six-year-old, who even a lad of twenty-one might fancy. And then she got up and said, 'It's me that's the haunted house, Harry. Everybody gets to be a haunted house in the end.' Then she added, 'I'll be glad if you can move out today. It never works a second time. I've tried it.'

And picking up her scarf and cardigan, she went off downstairs.

As he left, an hour later, he put his door key on the hall-stand and stood on the doormat and listened.

The house was silent. He couldn't tell if she was in or out.

He never went back to Brangwyn Gardens, and he never saw her again.

DOUBLE TAKE
June Oldham

When unemployed actress Olivia Quinn takes part in a small television news item about a missing girl, she triggers a series of dramatic events. Not only is she subjected to harassment, violence and prejudice, but events start to take on a disturbing similarity to those surrounding the missing girl's disappearance.

A SEAL UPON MY HEART
Pam Conrad

At the age of sixteen, Darcie suddenly becomes acutely aware of the lack of knowledge she has of her father. While her mother is away with her new husband, Darcie spends the summer playing detective to his whereabouts. She also finds friendship in the form of Roman, the seal-keeper at the zoo where she has a summer job. He charms her as if she is one of the animals, but is her infatuation with him perhaps going a little too far?

BIANCA
Joan Phipson

The first time they see her, Emily and Hubert catch no more than a glimpse of the girl's terrified face as she and her rowing boat loom briefly out of the mist, before it disappears back across the water. But it's a face which haunts them both and they quickly become deeply involved with this strange girl and her mysterious past.

OVERLORD
Christopher Hudson and Stuart Cooper

Tom Beddows, a young infantryman, writes in his diary of the true horror of war. The brutal training, the boredom and the sudden fear, the pity and the panic and most of all – the constant presence of death.

A sensitive, yet grim, story of one ordinary fighting man's experience of the greatest conflict in world history.

The book of the award-winning film of the same title.

THE ROAD TO MEMPHIS
Mildred D. Taylor

1941. All America is filled with rumblings of war in Europe and the Pacific. But Cassie Logan has reason to be more concerned with trouble back home in Mississippi. In this new story about the Logan family, Cassie is finishing high school in the city of Jackson and dreaming of college and law school. But no amount of schooling could prepare her for the tense dramas that are about to converge: a quarrel between two young lovers; a black friend's rage at his white tormentors and white youth's remorse over his part in a violent incident.

Caught up in the centre, Cassie is propelled into three harrowing, exhilarating, unforgettable days that force her to confront the adult world as never before.

MIGHTIER THAN THE LIPSTICK
Ed. Susan Adler

Astute, poignant and sensitive, this is a selection of stories by women from across the globe. There's the agony of dieting, a new look at the relationship between Ms Snow White and the seven dwarfs, the pain of losing a child and the freshness of an eager young woman arriving in a new city.

Including stories by Rosario Ferré, Margaret Sutherland, Ravinder Randhawa, Kate Pullinger and Leonora Brito, this international collection of stories provides a stimulating introduction to the wealth of women's writing today.